HUNGRY

A Random Isolated Event

Newly revised and edited

ERICK
T.
RHETTS

HUNGRY

HUNGRY

Also, by Erick T. Rhetts

LOST ON SKINWALKER RANCH

THE MULEDEER CHRONICLES

SOPHIA

SKINWALKER RANCH:
IN THE SHADOW OF THE RIDGE

THE AIRFIELD

REVELATIONS: END

THE SHADOW WALKERS

Available on Amazon and Create Space

HUNGRY

Published by Prensa Tinta Azul

Copyright © 2016 by Erick T. Rhetts

Published in the United States of America

Cover by Erick T. Rhetts

HUNGRY

HUNGRY

Predators and Prey

The alpha male stood within the cover of the rocks, waiting as the stragglers from his clan made their way through the narrow pass. These were the older and weaker ones, tiring and slowing and starting to stumble. The younger and stronger ones were already long strides ahead. The dominant males still moved quickly and with ease.

The young females, too, he noticed, were equally as fierce. First to pass were those with new-born infants, holding them tight to their hearts. Then came those with small ones, each clinging to their mother's back, their long spindly legs wrapped at the hip and thin arms slung around the neck, their eyes serious and their expression without fear. Then came the females soon to birth, refusing to lag behind.

The pursuit, nonetheless, even before this last sprint, had been closing, and this well beyond the point where in the past they would have given up.

The alpha had led his clan this way many times before, and always when being hunted. Here the surface underfoot was soft and unstable, which slowed the pursuit. But not his kind. Having but two toes on each foot, they were able to shift direction without thinking, their sleek and agile frames remaining centered and upright.

The images that came to his eyes, distant and indistinct in the pale amber light, found no recollection. Nevertheless, he was resigned to push on. There was no other action. They'd either lose the pursuit here among the tall stone formations, the twisting gullies, and the holes to crawl into or, surely, they all would all be

6

HuNGRY

slain. Already the scent of so many had been lost, though he didn't know to count.

He kept his eyes ahead, watching as his clan moved deeper into the rocks, further than they had ever gone before, the short, dense cilia-like hair covering their bodies, head to toe, catching and refracting the amber half-light and making them near invisible, little more than a shimmer of vague movement against the static backdrop.

But his experience taught him that these predators could be fooled only so long. As soon as they cut down the distance, even that shimmer would be enough to give them away. Predators, too, could learn.

He glanced back the way they had come, his eyes searching for something matching the simple sketch in his mind: the predators were big—two, maybe three of his kind together, moving down on all-fours, not upright, their necks thick and long, their faces elongated and muzzled, and always they pursued in packs. He turned and tilted his head, holding his breath and listening. Silent hunters, these that followed, they nonetheless would soon give their approach away, incapable of concealing the high-pitched squeal and whining that accompanied the anticipation of the kill.

At first, he saw and heard nothing, the unease twitching the long, sleek muscle bellies of his limbs diminishing just slightly. Finally, he had a notion that the chase may have been abandoned. Perhaps their pursuers had lost the scent, or maybe the expenditure of energy was no longer worth the prize.

But just as he started to turn, intent on catching up with his clan, to lead them to a place of shelter, he caught movement out of the corner of his eye. The predators had changed tactics, no longer following in the wake of the clan, but instead taking to the granite-like surface of the ridge above. No longer relying on scent or visual

HUNGRY

contact, they were simply continuing, perhaps mindlessly, perhaps strategically, in a direction from which there was no turning. Regardless, their number was greater than the alpha would have thought possible; they were too close to outrun; and they were moving fast.

He didn't wait around to see if he had been noticed, resigned that despite how tired the members of his clan were, how hungry, they were going to have to fight. And they were going to die.

The alpha ran effortlessly, aware of the tug just behind his left knee and a bit of a burn below his rib cage. He ignored them both and pushed on. In short order, he came upon a pair of old ones. He passed them by without stopping. They had been reduced to a hobbling stride and would be the next to die.

Out ahead of him was an open expanse of low round-topped dunes, one giving away to another, and beyond which appeared to be a second ridge, curving into the horizon and down into a gulley. Everything was in differing shades of amber, draped with the shadows of half-light. To his left, the outer ridge tapered inward, narrowing and dropping like a ramp, funneling the pursuing predators down and across the clan's only means of escape. It would be a race.

He darted out of the last of the concealing stone formations, across a narrow band of rock and onto the sand. Up an over the first dune, he came down the other side where three more of the old ones had decided they'd go on no further. Two were females, one a male. He was still large and his arms and legs strong, but he had gone soft in the belly and his back was not the good kind of wide. His eyes, too, had lost the deep, dark yellow of youth, now closer to opaque and dull, but with no sign of fear. He'd fight one more time, and death would come to him quickly, and to the

8

females he'd try to defend. They exchanged glances and nothing more.

Relying on instinct alone, the alpha climbed and descended one dune after the other, all the while the ridge to his left closing in on the escape and bringing the predators down into their midst. He saw, too, the second ridge, the way to safety, before him growing larger, the path at its base dropping down into the gulley, and then the gulley into the canyon.

He passed the old ones by, the weak ones, huddled together in groups of two or three, until there were no more to pass. One more dune and he was with a quick burst of speed at the backs of his fighters. They had strategically fallen back, allowing the females and children to outpace them, to go on ahead.

Sensing the presence of the alpha, the other males slowed to a jog, let him get before them, then as one they veered from their path, intent on cutting-off the descent of the predators. There was no sense of victory, no sense of survival. There was only delay: occupy the predators long enough to allow the females and young ones to escape through the gulley. There they could hide among the fissures slicing through the walls of the canyon, crawl into the tight, dark caverns where the bigger predators couldn't follow.

Down the ridge the predators came, more in number than the alpha had ever seen in one place. Down into the dunes they came, their movements slowed by the shifting sand. As if planned, a small group broke off from the whole, immediately wheeling away toward the stragglers. Perhaps the predators, too, had their weaker ones, and it were these that were permitted the easier prey.

There was no strategy, there was no plan. This was not a hunt where the alpha would make the first move and everyone else would follow, each fulfilling his role as every member of the clan had done since first there was a clan. There was no circling this time, no turning the prey into the pursuit, no closing ranks, no going for the back of the neck and holding until help came. This was throwing yourself at a predator, allowing the desperate will to live to summon whatever strength and tenacity there was to summon, and then fighting to certain death as to provide precious seconds to ensure the survival of the clan.

The first attack by the clan members took the predators by surprise. Prey doesn't attack predator. Unaccustomed to the loose sand at their feet, and incapable of finding foothold, the results were unpredictable. The clan came down upon the predators from the tops of the dunes, launching themselves recklessly for the back of their thick necks. Fingers long and with razor sharp nails punctured deep into flesh, drawing forth ribbons of dark, viscous blood. But little damage was done, at best, managing only to trip up some of the predators so that others stumbled and went down, too.

Flung from the neck of the largest of the predators, the alpha went shoulder first into the dune, the sand swallowing his arm to the elbow and pooling in around his chin. Within an instant, he was back on his feet, whirling in anticipation of attack. Instead, his eyes fell to the clan member he knew to be in all but social stations his equal: there were no names among them, only station. His teeth and claws were sunk into the neck of a predator, just below its muzzle. But at the same time, two other predators had separate hold on the clan member, one its powerful jaw closed on his side and the other tearing into the rounded muscle belly at the back of his leg.

The alpha prepared to spring, to throw himself into the fray. But just then, the clan member let go his bite on the predator's neck. His eyes rolled back and a gush of blood came from his mouth. His body then dropped limp to the sand, but only for a moment. The predator, released from the grip, turned in a blurred motion and drove its teeth into the clan member's exposed neck. As if choreographed, all three predators gave a fierce tug of their heads and necks. The body of the clan member contorted grotesquely and then came apart, the innards spilling forth and blood splattering the predators, muzzle and shoulders.

Similar scenes were repeating themselves everywhere the alpha looked.

It was then that a high-pitched squeal rose thinly above the snarls and yips of the attack. The alpha recognized the distressed call of his female.

Responding to the pull of their kind, the alpha turned and head at full speed in the direction of the cry. He was not alone. Others, too—those that could manage to elude the predators, were upon his heels.

In frenzied feeding, the predators were slow to react, and pursuit was slow to come.

Up and over one dune after the next, the alpha and what remained of the males of his clan closed the distance to the gulley, well out-pacing any pursuers who might be following. None turned to look.

Down the slope of the last line of dunes, they came out onto a flat expanse of broken rock and down into a v-shaped gulley. There, just before the way down into the canyon widened, what remained of the females and young ones had managed to clamber up into the rocks where the predators could not reach. The bodies of the others lay here and there, brought down and slaughtered, but not yet fed upon, as the predators sought to have at the rest.

There was no thought process involved. The alpha charged down the slope of the dune and straight at the nearest predator, crouched back upon its hind quarters and head turned. There was no intent to kill, only to distract. A body length from the predator, the alpha launched himself. Hurtling through the empty air, he drove his shoulder into the nape at the back of the predator's head and wrapped his arms around to the front of its neck in a choke hold. It was a precarious advantage he kept only briefly. With a powerful twist of its head, the predator shook him off. He was sent skittering and spinning across the hard ground, crashing into the base of the rock upon which the remnant of his clan had refuge.

But he was not alone. The other clan males followed his lead. Most were not as lucky as he, knocked down and set upon, the powerful jaws clamped down upon their throats while others tore at their soft and exposed extremities.

Up to his feet in an instant, the alpha spied a foothold in the rock. As the predators came at him, eyes intense and teeth bared, he leaped towards it with his left foot. Finding a narrow ledge and catching its edge, he launched himself upward. Arms out ahead of him, he caught enough of the face of the rock to scramble up, found a second edge with his right foot, and with a burst of strength held in reserve, scrambled atop, just out of the reach of the snapping jaws. Others had managed the same, but much fewer than had started out.

The predators, not to be denied, split into two groups and spread out, the first looking for a way up into the rock, and the second going deeper into the gulley and doubling-back along a narrow ledge descending towards the clan. They were trapped.

Suddenly, a thunderous boom shook the stone. A darkness, shades of pale amber, roiled overhead. Rolls of thunder began off in the distance and sped nearer. One after the other and in quick succession they exploded. Flashes of dark amber lighting crackled downward, searing the canyon walls with lashes of fire. A rumbling wave of sound grew from the rock, echoing down the length of the canyon before turning back upon itself.

Predator and prey alike threw themselves flat to the ground.

Sheaths of darkness started raining from the sky. Like cascading panes of amber-reflecting glass, their ragged edges glinted with trails of fire, gold and yellow. Fast and sudden like slithering snakes, they extinguished themselves on the stone floor only to fire up again along the edges of the ridge, or along the walls or beneath the rocky eaves. Sheet after sheet rained down and exploded into silent puddles of liquid sparks, spreading out like water rings and ebbing into sudden darkness.

Startled, the predators froze in their steps. As the intensity of the storm increased, the sheaths of chaotic energy shattering against the walls of stone, they panicked, trying to turn back on the narrow edge, and one after the other falling to the surface below. Flopped to the stone, they couldn't get back on their feet fast enough, flailing against a footing they couldn't find, splaying out wide and awkwardly with limbs going this way and that, rolling and scrambling.

In an instant decision based on no particular reasoning, the alpha male took two long strides across the top of the rock and dove head first into the falling sheets of vivid darkness. An incredibly intense brightness flared across his eyes. His ears filled with a deafening cacophony of sounds, none of which he recognized. And then everything went black.

But for a fraction of a second.

Then everything was enveloped in a blinding flare of heatless white, so much so that it distracted the alpha to the realization that his feet were momentarily pedaling in empty space. Then he dropped, the ground coming up to meet his feet before he was ready. His ankles gave way, first one and then the other, his knees bending with a jolt, and his upper body pitched forward. Down upon his face he went, his extended snout rubbing hard across a spongy surface for which he had no recollection, and something else which he imagined was sliding and slipping about. But the heatless flare of light remained disconcerting, and eyes squeezed closed, he started tumbling, first head over heels and then every which way, and unable to stop.

He was tumbling down a hillside, of this much he was aware. But everything else seemed displaced and alien. There were odors and smells confusing his nostrils, a taste to the air that was heavy and pushing against his lungs, and sounds filling his ears for which he found no recognition. And then his momentum was suddenly spent. He slid a short distance more and came to halt against something strong and hard. It wasn't rock or stone. He chanced opening his eyes, but again the heatless flare jabbed like thorns into his brain. He closed them again, and brought up his hands to grow the darkness. As he did, one of the clan members came crashing up against him, momentarily pressing him hard into the bark of the tree against which he rested, though he knew it not for a tree.

Then came another clan member, and then another, until there were eight in all, though the alpha knew not to count. Four were males, warrior and hunters; two were females, one with child; one was a young one who managed to stay alive; and he, the alpha, was eight.

Together they sat huddled, eyes squeezed closed all, and waited, the alien smells and sounds a rich assault from every side. But there was no fear, only waiting, only patience.

And then, though they knew it not, night came and the heatless flare of light was gone.

14

Damned Raccoons

The garbage pail went over with a thud, and Barry heard it. He cursed under his breath, and then aloud, "God-damned raccoons."

He slapped his newspaper down on the coffee table. As he did, the pen in his hand flipped from his fingers, bounced off of the wood floor and skittered over in the direction of the fireplace. He didn't quite see where.

"Where are my damned glasses?" He complained with no one there to hear.

Barry lived alone. Had done so since Mary, his wife, his second wife, passed away. "Second one I killed off," he commented at her wake, a misplaced chuckle. Those in attendance pretended not to take notice. He didn't think anything of it. As far as he was concerned, none of them had been invited, anyway. Where the fuck were they, he thought, when she was lying in bed, coughing up blood and shitting herself?

He tapped at the breast pocket of his flannel shirt. Didn't feel the glasses.

If they're not in my pocket, he thought, they're up on the mantle. He was in the habit of leaving them there whenever he went into the kitchen. Sure enough, that's where he saw them.

But he walked right past them and towards the corner of the parlor. Standing there barrel up was his shotgun, twelve gauge and loaded. Might be a bear.

He made towards the front door, his knees creaking every step of the way; and if they weren't, they might have well been the way they felt, the pain stabbing at him enough to be annoying.

HUNGRY

"Fuck me," he spit, realizing he had walked right past his glasses, without which, especially in the dark of the yard, he couldn't see a thing.

He went back for them, thinking it could have been worse: he might have realized after having gone down those damned porch steps.

The glasses were those thick rimmed kind with the extra bar at the bridge. He learned the hard way, having had them slide from his face God knew how many times after falling asleep in his recliner, usually after a snort or two too many, only to wake and find them twisted and broken, stuck between his hip and the cushion.

He put them on, decided the smudge in the middle of the right lens wasn't worth the effort to wipe away. Besides, it'd only make it worse. Those fucking cloths don't work for shit, he said. It's either wash them or leave'em be. He left the smudge.

Back at the front door, he turned the knob and pulled it toward him. The door opened reluctantly, dragging across the welcome mat he saw no reason for but left there all the same. He started to reach for the porch light, but decided better against it. Don't want to spook the critter, he thought. I want to shoot the bastard.

He pulled the screen door aside as quietly as he could. He knew it would give him away regardless. "Just like my knees," he drawled in a whisper as he eased off. Just another noise in the night, he convinced himself. Raccoons don't know a door from a falling branch.

He crossed the porch and down the stairs he went: one, two, and then the third.

He went down the walkway a stride or two, not that he wanted to go in that direction, but the shrubs out front had become so overgrown, it was the only way around. He then stepped from the pebbled surface to the grass, which too had grown taller than it should be. "Got to get the neighbor's kid to mow this shit," he said aloud, but not so much so as to give himself away.

The grass was wet and slippery, and Barry took care not to take a misstep that would send him sprawling. Pride was a personal thing. So dark or not, no one around to see or not, just the thought of winding up on his ass because he no longer could put one foot down after the other like a man would be enough to convince him it was time to put the barrel beneath his own chin.

The garbage pails were to the side of the house, there against the outside wall of the garage. Barry had plans of putting up a corral just for the purpose of keeping the critters out. Make it high enough and tight enough that they couldn't knock the pails over. He just hadn't found the time to get to it. Shaking his head and waving the shotgun, he reminded himself to make it a priority. There wasn't much worse, he thought, then picking broken eggshells, soggy coffee filters, or God knows what else from the ground—unless, of course, it was wiping sloppy shit from your dying wife's inner thigh. He shuttered, unwanted recall assaulting his nostrils with a sudden whiff of that sickly-sweet odor that comes from something dead and decaying.

He then realized, mid-step, that he actually was catching the scent of something. It wasn't sloppy shit, and it wasn't a dead thing. It was a musk. But not like randy livestock. No, there was plenty of that here in the valley. The neighbor with the kid had some cows and a bull, had some goats, too. Nothing more ridiculous, he thought, than a horny goat climbing up on the back of a bitch goat, the mating smells hanging in the air, or those God-damned bulls, horses even worse. Cock and shit.

And then the odor hit him again, snapping him back to the moment. It stank of an old dog, the kind of dog you just can't pet anymore without getting that stink all over your hands, and that oily shit—whatever that was. But no, this smell was sharper than that, heavier, too, with a density you could almost taste. It gave him the *Willies*.

He pictured one of those big raccoons, one of the big males, the ones that are as big as a dog, crazed from rabies, some maggot-filled and festering wound on its hind-quarters, and tearing mindlessly at his garbage, just waiting for an old idiot like him to come bumbling along. Hadn't he just read about some kid in the city on his way to school being attacked by a raccoon? The fucking thing jumped on his back and was clawing and chewing on the boy's face—and with the kid's mother standing right there.

He stopped mid-stride. Cursed himself for being such a pussy. "Where's your balls got to?" He admonished himself and gripped the shotgun a bit firmer, as if he was grabbing for assurance what remained of his own manhood. He lifted it waist high and moved forward.

The garage was to his immediate right. He decided to give it wide berth, come around the side so that he'd have a good line of sight. Rabid raccoon or not, it was getting an ass full of buckshot. Taking care to lift his feet up the best he could so as not to drag them and give himself away, he made it across the driveway without kicking pebbles every which way. He made for the far side of the walkway, on to the grass, just as tall and just as wet, angling wide to where the pails would come into view. He was prepared and stepped lightly.

No sooner did he get himself in position, the pails camouflaged by the dark, a sweep of humid night air hit him straight in the face. The thickness of that musky stench was so bad that it was all he could do to keep from gagging. He backed up a stride, and it was then that the dark against dark, to which his mind without giving it thought gave shape, suddenly gained a pair of reflecting eyes, large black dots in elongated fields of pale yellow.

It took his mind a second or two to register that it was no raccoon, and not a bear. It was the hiss of warning, and then the menace of a guttural growl, not loud but chilling, which caused his brain to scream and the too-late act of trying to get the gun elevated.

The thing was on him before he could get the barrel pointed. He never even felt the second one that slammed into his back. His throat had already been ripped out by then, the wheezing of his last breaths leaking through his exposed and ruptured windpipe. Paying no heed, the two creatures, long nails and teeth, shred greedily the flesh clinging unnecessarily to Barry's bones, gobbling down in chunks as much as they could before some other predator might come to claim a share.

HUNGRY

Put the Dog Out

Bob chided himself for even thinking it.

"Bob, put the dog out!"

At the time, perhaps, it was worth it. After all, Darla had the sweetest ass in school. It actually dumbfounded him that she said yes when he asked her to the prom, something he would never had done if the rest of the guys hadn't said he didn't have the balls.

He almost didn't, almost chickened-out. I mean, who the fuck am I, he thought at the time. Every guy in school wants a piece of that. Why would she even give me a second look?

Bob was Bob, and that was about the extent of it. Not that he wasn't at the time a good-looking guy—still was, some said. He had all that blonde hair, the blue eyes, that cute-boy next door thing going for him. But he wasn't a jock, wasn't a motor-head, wasn't one of those Emo-boys. Shit, he was just plain Bob.

He had to grin, thinking back on it. It was a Friday night back in January, senior year—1981. It was testing week, where the really smart kids took the state exams in advance, and the really dumb kids had to take them again after failing in the spring, some in the fall, too. With no classes, it was like party city, that whole week. But Friday night was cut-loose night. The guys, and that included the girls, especially the chicken-heads, would get together, not formally, the other side of the *hill* to drink and smoke. You drank whatever anyone brought—usually beer, but someone always managed a bottle or two, and smoked weed. There were always those two or three guys with cars willing to take a ride out of the valley, go either north or south into one of the white neighborhoods, or even the black ones, and make a buy. The guys would pool their money, some more than others, and get whatever they could get.

"Bob, do you hear me?"

Bob liked his pot, still did. Just like back then, he always had a bit of a stash, a rolled-up sandwich baggy with some bud, green and tight, and his small pipe.

He was buzzed that night, both on the drink and the smoke. Darla was there, just across the fire pit. She was sitting with some of her girlfriends, all of them pretty enough in their own way, whether it be the slim waist, the perky twins, the sensual curl of the lips, or the shape painted over by pants you'd have to be poured into. Not that you could see it just then, all bundled up as they were against the cold, snow from the last fall still here and there in patches on the ground between the trees, and the wind, finding its way around the boles, taking nips at exposed skin.

Stevie was sitting beside him, sipping from a beer, taking a hit when the joint made its way back around, and jolting him regularly with a knee to his thigh. Each jolt was accompanied by a quick glance in Darla's direction, and then that look that said, "Well, are you gonna?"

"Damn it, Bob, this dog is going to piss on my floor!"

That voice and that tone, it banged off Bob's forehead like a golf ball shot out of canon. He knew when he'd have to get up and put the dog out. The tone and the volume weren't there yet, and she hadn't yet taken a shot at him for being lazy or not getting his ass off the couch to help around here.

Bob could still feel Stevie's bony knee jabbing into him, as if he was there in the moment. He had been both high enough and drunk enough to do it. There was no ceremony, no preface, no build up. He simply spit it out right over the top of the fire and straight into Darla's pretty face. "Darla," he said, and as matter-of-fact as could be, "go to the prom with me." He didn't even bother to make it a question.

"Okay." That's what she said. Nothing more. Just, "Okay."

Things just kind of rolled from there.

He had had his share of dates up to that point. What boy in the valley didn't? Outnumbered by the ladies, there were only so many guys to go around. So, it was rare that, if asked, a girl would say no, at least the first time. At the worst, the girls would have something to gossip about and the guys could point to the date as proof they weren't gay.

But like most of the guys, despite what they'd say when they were together, he hadn't got past second base with any of them. He had managed to slip his hands up a shirt or two, got acquainted with a couple of palm-sized twins. One of the Murphy sisters had even given him a hand job. But it was in the dark, in the trees beyond the back fence of their property, and she wouldn't let him take it out. She complained afterwards about getting stuff on her hand, and he was left with wet spots on his boxers.

So, Darla was his first. And he was hers. It happened well before the prom.

The first time he saw her without clothes still stuck with him. It was a sight he wouldn't allow himself to forget. She was babysitting. He waited for the parents to pull out of the driveway and then he knocked. She acted like she wasn't expecting him, but she had to at least given it some thought. What else was he supposed to do?

Of course, she let him in, not one word of her scolding or protest in earnest. Her charge was an infant, and already tucked away for the evening. They sat together on the couch, watching some television. It was coincidence only that the movie had some adult scenes, and instead of feeling awkward about it, they both got the idea at the same time. It started with some kissing and went from there. It was she who pulled down his zipper, and not the other way around.

But she didn't want to do it on the couch. "What if someone walks in?" She said, as if she really believed it would happen that way.

She made him wait out there in the living room while she went into a second bedroom. A guestroom, she had called it. "Don't come in until I tell you to."

He promised.

She gave the word, and he went in. She was beneath the covers of a twin-sized bed. He saw her clothes piled on an easy chair there in the corner but an arm's length a way, so he knew she was naked. He was unsure if he should shed his clothes right there in front of her, maybe just to his boxers, and then crawl in beside her. Seeing the expectation in her eyes, he went for it, doffing it all right there. He didn't give a second thought to the fact that he was already excited, or that she might be surprised by how much there was to him. She was.

"Oh, my God!" She said with a smile.

He felt a bit self-conscious at the moment, and slid in beside her. She lifted the covers as he did so, and he saw for the first time her every line. His first impression was how small she really was, and he wondered if he'd hurt her.

"Jesus, Bob. Do I have to do everything myself?"

Whatever excitement he was feeling at the moment—and there was a bit of a stir, he lost it all as that voice jabbed into his skull.

"Alright already, I heard you. Can't a man get a minute around here?"

They did it three times that night, right there in the guest bed. The first time, she positioned herself on him. He felt her hand as she guided him, and then he was inside. He did little more after that than rise up to meet her, and even then, as gently as he could. He watched her face the whole time, but she seemed to be elsewhere most of it, only occasionally touching his eyes with hers. It was over rather quickly, but neither one of them seemed to mind. The second time, he lay on top of her, worried that his weight was too much for her. But she didn't complain. This time, too, he was longer and stronger, and with one hand down on the bed on each side of her, like he was doing push-ups or something. She had a grimace on her face throughout, so intense that it drove him on. They went on much longer than the first, and this time, she felt it, too. He rolled off to one side, and they clung to each other for seemingly eternity. The third time, she wrapped her legs around his back. But the baby cried before they could finish, and by the time she got back to him, the look on her face told him that there'd be no more, not tonight.

She had glanced over at the clock as if to make it official. "It won't do to have you here when they get home."

"You know what? Since you can't get your lazy ass of that couch, I'm just going to open the back door and let him out."

"Fuck, Darla. I said I was coming."

But all he heard after that was, "Don't bother." And then the back door opening.

He looked around to find where he had left his shoes. They were all the way over by the front door, down at the end of the foyer. "I said I was coming." He was tempted to go in his socked feet. Grass would be wet, even if the rain had come down only for a bit.

He had just got the second shoe on when he heard the high-pitched screech and a whole bunch of barking and a sharp yip. His first thought was the dog had cornered a raccoon. They screeched

24

like that when they were spooked, and the dog yipped like that when he got swatted or bit.

"Damn it, Darla. I told you I was coming." Now he was going to have to pull the damn dog away from a raccoon, and if the thing was cornered, it could get ugly.

He strode into the kitchen at the back of the house, his face all set with that look shit like this brought out of him. But Darla wasn't there. He made for the door which led out to the backyard. The back light was on. The dog pen was to the left and maybe ten yards from the house. Bob saw immediately that the gate was open. There was no sign of either Darla or the dog, and the night was silent.

"Darla, where are you?" He called out, thinking she wouldn't have gone far. This was not the petite thing he thought he'd break that night. Four grown children and a fondness for late night snacking had changed all of that. This had become a woman who complained whenever she had to go too far back down an aisle at the supermarket after forgetting something she had on the list.

He stopped and listened. There was a steady breeze in the trees at the edge of the property, and then, too, going up the hill. As much as he wanted to turn around and go back into the house, he knew he'd never hear the end of it. Darla couldn't get enough of telling him it was his dog. Why they needed to have a dog now that the kids were grown and out of the house was beyond her. "It's not like you need a companion," she had said when he brought the pup home. "You got me."

He remembered putting the shepherd mix down on the floor, and then making some kind of comment about how much there was of her to have. She had gotten that big. But before she could tell him to go fuck himself, or whatever it was she would have come back with, the little fellow had already pissed beside the table leg. Her fondness for the dog never did get any better.

No doubt, Ruff had chased out after the coon, and Darla had gone to fetch him back. Bob gave a thought to which direction, and then settled on up the hill. Where else would a coon go but for the trees. Before setting off, he gave a thought to locking the backdoor. But then again, he didn't have his keys with him, and besides, the front door wasn't locked either. He shrugged. "It's the valley. Who's going to bother?"

So, he went off, across the length of the back yard and towards the far side of the house, making for the path that went up the hill and between the trees. No sooner did he turn the corner, the side yard coming into view, he saw in the pale light coming through the windows on that side of the house two dark figures bent towards the ground. All he could tell from first glance was that they were both pretty big, meaning not so close to the ground as to be dogs, or coyotes, but not big enough to be bears, or even people. And there was a stink to the air, like skunk, or something moldy and dank. They were making slurping noises, between which there were muted snarls and what sounded to him like wet cloth or tissue tearing.

He looked around for something to throw. But as he did, first the one and then the other became aware of his presence, lifting their heads from whatever they were doing and turning towards him. They were so black against the dark that all he saw were large black dots in elongated fields of pale yellow, as if their eyes were reflecting that light coming from his windows.

A primal fear gripped Bob's innards. It was like nothing he had ever felt before. His legs turned to jelly and his first step came with a wobble. With no warning at all, the two things came at him with a quickness seemingly surreal. The flight or fight thing took him before he knew it, and without another thought, he was in full stride, not back towards the house, but up the hill. He didn't know it at the time, but it actually saved his life; a third one was coming at him from that very direction. And just as the three of them converged at his back, Ruff came out of nowhere, tearing down past Bob and leaping into their midst. Bob gave no thought going back to the dog's defense, and instead ran up the hill as fast as his forty-eight-year-old legs could carry him.

It was only when he heard Ruff growl and yip for that one last time, and he so many strides away, did he stop to consider it couldn't have been anything other than Darla, or what was left of her, that those things were bent over and devouring. His guilt for thinking of leaving her, leaving her with the house, and leaving the valley, looking for something else, for something new, stopped him in his tracks, if but for a moment. "No use going back," he told himself. "Nothing I can do now." Convinced, he went on, listening to the darkness, listening for pursuit.

Get to the other side of the hill, he told himself. Get to the neighbors and call the sheriff. That's what he had to do.

27

HUNGRY

Sylvan Road

Lisa gave the boy the three dollars she had folded in her hand, closed the door to the back seat of the Grand Cherokee. It bothered her a little that for the life of her, she couldn't recall the name that went with the boy. He was definitely one of Alba Torres' boys. Even if she hadn't known that right off, there weren't any other Hispanic families here in the valley. Her husband, Abel, was Mexican, and besides, he had his mother's looks. She was what you'd call a handsome woman, and so was the boy—handsome, that is. Those deep brown eyes, the dark complexion, the easy-on-the-eyes features. Emil was the oldest boy; she remembered that much. But he was in college, at least a year already, maybe even two. Then there was Peter. But he was the youngest of the boys. This was the one in the same grade as her own son, Andy. Or maybe he was a year older, 15 maybe, if he was working already. Not that it mattered too much in the valley. Guy, the owner of the food mart, had said as much, offering Andy a job if he wanted it, when the summer first started. He would have taken it, too. But she thought, as mothers often do, that he should enjoy his summer. There was plenty of time for working later.

She turned to say good night, but Alba's boy was already at the door of the store, slipping the folded bills into his pants pocket. She wondered if it was enough, or did the boy think she was cheap. It was only four bags, she rationalized. Only two trips, and short ones at that. She found her keys and walked around to the other side of the Cherokee.

The black Jeep made the turn out of the small parking lot, Lisa looking both ways before pulling out onto the single lane roadway—two, if you count both directions. There was no one coming, no headlights. Not that she expected there would be, not at this time of night. She smiled. If Guy wasn't familiar with her routine, as he was with just about everyone in the valley, he probably would have closed by now. The small-town thing, at least, she had to admit, was one of the perks to all this isolation.

She made the right and headed towards home, to the east side of the hill, saw over her shoulder the lights to the store go dark.

It bothered her, too, that her children were home by themselves. It made it a little easier on her, though, that Andy was now fourteen and Maggie sixteen. She didn't have to worry about them playing with matches and setting the house on fire or letting strangers into the house—not that that was ever much of a concern in the valley. There weren't any strangers. Now if she could only be certain that Maggie's increasing interest in the boys at school didn't extend to having any of them over when mom wasn't home.

Lisa could understand if it was one boy in particular, teen love and all that. But not for Maggie. She wasn't interested in focusing on just one. She told Lisa as much in passing conversation. Nothing promiscuous about it was what she took from it, more like an infatuation with the gender.

"Some of them are really cute," Maggie had said, as if she was talking about puppies or shoes. "I just like talking to them, watching their expressions, how their features change when they smile or laugh, or get really serious, and even embarrassed sometimes." She grinned, a bit sheepishly, when confessing, "I get a big kick out of the ones that get all shy when they talk to girls. The ones that don't hang out with the other cool guys, or play sports, or get the attention of the cougar-ettes. You know, the senior girls that like to tease the underclassmen." She nodded,

29

then, an expression to match. "The shy ones, I think I like them the best. They're more sincere and genuine."

It was an assessment which surprised Lisa, and made her proud of her daughter at the same time.

She asked Maggie if she liked those other ones, too. The popular ones, the ones the other girls do pay attention to.

Maggie shrugged, as if there was any need to ask. She grinned mischievously. "They're the ones with the nice butts and the muscles."

Lisa had given her that look that mothers give their daughters at moments like those.

"Come on, mom," Maggie said giving her that *as if you never did look.* "But it's not only that. When you're alone with guys like that—not all of them, they can be really vulnerable. They tell you and say things they won't tell or say to anyone else. I think that's really cool."

Lisa thought it was as good a time as any to have that mother and daughter talk. She was pleasantly surprised when Maggie went with it, listening to what a mother says when talking about such things, and responding when she wanted in a way that Lisa had to look twice to be sure it was Maggie she was talking too.

The recollection gave her confidence that Maggie wasn't letting any of them in through the back door or her bedroom window while Andy was distracted, doing his homework at the kitchen table or playing video games online with his friends. How she had pushed out two such different kids, she often wondered.

But not really. Andy was like his father, she knew. Quiet and reserved, but smart, oh, so smart. He had his dad's looks, too: the sandy brown hair, the boyish face with the gentle features, small nose, and the thin lips with that serious look—even when his brown eyes were smiling. He was lean, too, like his dad, with an

30

athletic build—with little interest in athletics, and soon to probably be as tall, though presently he was small for his age. She knew it bothered him, some, being one of the smallest in his class. But he always perked up when she assured him his dad was that way, too, and he made it to six feet and one inch, two when he wore shoes.

Andy didn't know his dad the way fourteen-year old boys get to know their fathers. He had passed when Andy was seven, almost eight. Doctor or no, there was nothing Lisa could do about that. The cancer was so aggressive. It came like an owl sweeping out of a tree in the darkness, plucking him from the earth as if he was a white mouse perched atop a red rock poking above the grass. It was so quick, the way the cancer took him, a day or two short of six weeks, that he had time to do more than wriggle one or twice in its claws. Then, just like that, he was gone, and they were alone, she and Maggie and Andy. And that's the way it had been since.

The darkness of the unlighted road brought her back to her original line of thought: the late shift.

One of only two doctors at the clinic, not counting the intern, Lisa had long ago accepted the fact that someone had to take the late shift. So, she and Dr. Dave—that's what everyone called him—took turns, one month on, next month off. They agreed a month allowed for some degree of acclimation, and ultimately made the transition easier on their schedules.

This happened to be her month on. It meant leaving the house at noon and getting back home after dark, and if lucky—like she was tonight, before ten. Taking a quick glance over at the clock, she saw it was only a few minutes after nine.

The clinic was a big deal in the valley. It was both health care and dental care. In fact, it was any kind of care when it came to treating people in the valley for whatever it was that needed treatment. They did everything there short of major surgery. For that, you had to go to the city. And that meant going up or down 87, north to Plattsburg or south towards Albany or Schenectady, or somewhere in between. Which also meant if the malady was really serious, if they couldn't treat it there at the clinic, and unless the EMTs were really good and you not on death's doorstep, you probably weren't going to make.

Driving as if on automatic pilot, and looking without really seeing, whatever it was came out of nowhere, moving from the shoulder of the road to her right and across her path. Reacting to a sudden squirt of adrenalin, she hit the brakes. The back of the Cherokee came up faster than the front was slowing and the Jeep fish-tailed to the right. She both heard and felt the contact off the front of the Jeep and to the fender on her side, so quick the thing was moving. It was just a muted thud though. Whatever critter it was, she hadn't hit it square on nor all that solidly.

The vehicle came to a stop some thirty yards from the point of impact, the front end angled to face into the trees to her left, but thankfully with all four tires still on the paved surface. Her heart repeatedly fisting against her sternum, she allowed herself a moment to calm down. She took deep slow breaths, let them out slowly. Her whole body felt as if clenched, her hands clutching the steering wheel tighter than when she let her kids talk her into taking that roller coaster ride on Coney Island.

She opened the door a tad, the night wasting no time in laying a damp blanket of humid air over her exposed skin. Before committing a foot to the ground, she took a moment to listen, peering the while into the trees along the shoulder of the road. The Town Board saw no reason to put street lights this far out of town, so the odds of Lisa seeing anything at all, never mind a wild animal, weren't favorable. Nevertheless, her practical nature got the better of her, and she thought, at the very least, she'd get out and check the damage to the front end.

Leaving the door open, she first walked towards the back of the Jeep, relying on the pale glow of the rear lights reflecting off the ghostly haze to see if she could make out anything there, or perhaps off upon the shoulder. The light didn't allow for much distance, and there was nothing within its sphere, black against black, to suggest an animal of any kind. She dismissed the idea of walking any further from the vehicle, figuring that whatever it was she hit, if it had gone down, it wouldn't be back in the direction from which she came before she hit it. So, she went back towards the sweep of the headlights. Sure enough, there was a wrinkle on the fender—above the tirewell—and to the upper part of the bumper. Part of the frame around the headlight had been damaged, too. But other than that, nothing all that bad. It confirmed her suspicion that she hadn't caught it solid.

Noting the wash of the headlights as it fanned out before her, across the surface of the road, then the narrow swath of grass before the trees, and then the trees themselves, she decided it wouldn't do any harm to go as far as the trees and see if there was anything to see. She took only a handful of strides before the rank odor hit her. At first it was just a whiff, and then it was as if someone ran up and crammed her nostrils with fetid stink. It was the odor of decay, like that of a dead thing, but somehow equally as different. It made her uneasy, even afraid. She stopped dead in her tracks and then immediately started backing up, not taking her eyes from the black trunks of the trees before her. Maybe it was only a deer, she thought. But even so, out here dead things brought predators, coyotes or black bears. It didn't make much sense to walk right up to one or the other.

33

HUNGRY

A stride from the car, Lisa heard the unmistakable sound of branches and brush snapping under foot. Whatever it was, the light from the headlights caught the glint of its eyes. She hesitated only long enough to make out two elongated fields of pale yellow, each with a large dot of black somewhat to the middle. With no explanation for the sudden dread which threatened to handover control of her bowels, she covered the two steps between her and the front seat as fast as she could, pulling the door closed hard to her side and jabbing down on the button which locked them all. Staring out over the steering wheel, her peripheral vision lost along with her nerve, she saw nothing but the beam of the headlights and the dark shape of the trees. Whatever it was that had been out there only a second before, it was gone now.

Before putting the Cherokee in gear, Lisa took a moment to admonish herself for getting all worked up over animals in the woods. She then put the Jeep in reverse, backed into the lane so that it was facing properly forward, then shifted into drive, and pressing down evenly on the gas pedal made for home.

As she did, two figures emerged from beneath the trees, one moving less ably than the other, and followed in her direction.

HUNGRY

Grocery Bags

Andy moved his fingertips across the keyboard punching in his next move. He then launched and waited for his opponent to respond. He had been meeting Kyle to play online religiously for almost a year now, same time three nights a week. They had since been chatting between games, talking about the usual things boys their age talked about, but mainly school and girls, and of course, the game. In person, the two had never met, if you don't count webcam. Kyle lived in southwestern Ohio. Andy had never been to Ohio.

The screen flashed bright and then everything tumbled. Kyle, it seemed, had no answer for Andy's strategy. Game over. "My game," Andy typed into the field. Hit send.

A short moment later, Kyle responded. "I didn't expect that." His face filled the screen. He was smiling, his handsome features framed by dark black hair, tight to the ears, but then long and straight to the back and to the nape. His eyes, even with the limitations of the webcam, were a vibrant green with a sparkle like glass. His nose was slightly upturned, almost elfish, and his lips thin and straight, his cheek bones high and graceful. If Kyle was a girl, thought Andy, when they first connected visually, he guessed that the word *pretty* would fit. But that wasn't something Andy would ever say aloud. Stuff like that always got around somehow, and the last thing he needed was every guy in school thinking he was gay.

"I didn't think you'd have an answer for that," he said, the two of them now talking instead of typing.

"This time, yeah. But now you'll have to come up with something else. That shit only works one time."

Andy smiled. He knew Kyle was right. That's the way these kinds of games worked; but that's what made it so cool to play, also. You always had to be thinking. "Don't worry, I will."

Kyle changed the subject. "So, what do you got going on tonight? Anything?"

Andy shrugged. "Nothing. You have no idea how dead it is around here. I mean, we're in the middle of nowhere. I've told you we're in the middle of a valley, right?"

He saw Kyle sit back in the desk chair. "Can't be all that bad."

"Oh no? That's what you think. There's like a half-dozen kids my age around here, and when I say around here, I mean, like, just about the whole valley. And my house is like a million miles away from my closest friend."

"A million? That's pretty far. What are you on Mars?"

"Might as well be. I live on the other side of what everyone around here calls the *Hill*."

"I thought you said you lived in a valley?"

"We do. But, duh, you can't have a valley without hills. The ones here split the valley into two parts. We're out in the middle of bum-fucked Egypt."

Kyle started laughing. "Bum-fucked Egypt? I don't think I've heard that one before."

Andy found himself laughing, too. That and self-conscious with the sudden awareness of how much attention he was giving to Kyle's expressions, the sparkle to his eyes, him there on his screen, almost as if he was there in person. His feelings confused him to the point of distraction and he didn't catch what Kyle had just said to him.

"Can you still hear me?" He heard instead.

He shook his head once and blinked. "Yeah, sorry. I was distracted. My sister's in the other room." He covered.

36

HUNGRY

"Is she hot?"

"Who? My sister?"

Kyle leaned in towards the webcam. Raising his eyebrows a couple of times, he said, "Yeah. Not as a sister. As a girl, you know?" He cupped his hands at his chest.

"Man, I don't know. She's my sister. It's not like I look."

Kyle screwed up his mouth and smirked. He looked over his shoulder, and then leaned into towards the camera again, his face filling the screen. "C'mon man, I got a sister, too. You trying to tell me you never tried to catch a look? You know, peeking while she's in the shower, shit like that."

Andy performed the same safety check, looking over one shoulder and then the other. He, too, then leaned in closer to the camera lens. His voice took on a tone of conspiracy. "A couple of weeks ago, I walked in on her while she was sitting on the bowl. She went off like crazy, pulling down on her shirt to cover up, and all that. She called me a pervert. Man, I didn't even know she was in there. I thought she had gone out."

"So, what did you see?"

"I didn't see anything. Just her sitting there."

"Was she doing number one or number two?"

Andy scrunched up his brow. "I don't know. I didn't stick around long enough to find out."

Kyle chuckled. "You think they shit the same way we do?"

"Why? Is there a different way?"

Their conversation went on in the same direction for a while longer, Andy learning more about Kyle's sister than he wanted to, including just about every opportunity Kyle had to see her in various stages of undress. He couldn't imagine going to the extremes Kyle had gone, thinking the whole idea of invading his sister's privacy just not right.

37

Finally, he found the opportunity to get off the subject, getting around to asking Kyle what his particular plans were for the night.

He was disappointed when Kyle said nothing.

"I'm here talking with you. A friend of mine was supposed to come over, and then we were going to go hang out. But he got in some trouble with his parents, and they won't let him out. I don't know what he did; he wouldn't tell me. Said it was something stupid, and his parents were making too big a thing about it. Whatever."

Andy nodded. "If I wanted to go to a friend's house, I'd have to get my mother to drive me, and then pick me up afterwards. Most of them aren't valley kids. They live over by the school. It's all the way in the other direction, away from the hill."

"How many hills are there?"

Andy smiled. "I guess that is confusing. Anything that's outside of the valley is considered the other side of the hill. But everyone in the valley calls the part where I live *the hill*. If you can picture it, we have only one main road, Sylvan Road. You can see it on Map Quest, if you want. It kind of goes east to west, from the highway outside of the valley, then down into the valley and towards the hill where I live. It then goes up the hill a piece and wraps around to the other side, into the local streets. You then come out again, back on to Sylvan and back to the main highway.

"Where my house is, Sylvan cuts the hill into two parts—kind of. My house is at the base of the lower part. Then there's the road. Then on the other side of the road, the hill climbs up again. There's nothing but woods up that way. Then towards the top, there's the old burial grounds. That part is the real hill, where all the kids go to party and hang out. Though not into the burial grounds. No one really goes there, except maybe on a dare, or something like that.

HUNGRY

"Anyway, basically there's one way into the valley and one way out; unless you count the dirt trails back in the woods. If you have a good four-wheel drive, you can make it out west, over the top of the hill and down the other side. There're a few towns out that way and some State land.

"We don't have any schools here in the valley. Even the elementary school is on the other side. There's nothing here but a general store, a post office, the clinic where my mother works, and a couple of farm stands. In fact, that's the biggest thing around here: there's a bunch of farms and some orchards. Most of the houses around here have pretty big properties, but a lot of it is uphill and there's trees everywhere. It's cool if you're into running around in the woods, playing chase. There are all kinds of trails, and even some small caves. Not the kind that go back deep into the mountains, not like that. But the kind that are like underground. Pretty cool stuff to explore. You can also go hunting; it's all legal on your own property and up in the woods. There are deer, wild turkey, rabbits, squirrels, pretty much any kind of animal you'd want to shoot and eat."

Kyle was impressed. "That sounds cool. Do you have your own gun?"

Andy told a bit of a white lie. "I have my father's guns. There are two rifles. One is a thirty-aught-six, I think it's called. Then there's a .22 I use for small stuff, like squirrels and rabbits. My friend uses a shotgun for the turkeys, 20 gauge. You've got to extract the buckshot before you can eat them, but you don't need to be so accurate when shooting."

Andy left out the part about his mother not allowing him to use them.

Kyle said something then, but Andy was distracted by the sound of his mother's Jeep coming up the driveway, headlights

39

HUNGRY

bright against the front of the house. "I got to go, Kyle. My mom just pulled up."

Kyle nodded. "Cool, Andy. I'll hook up with you tomorrow. But you better come up with a new move, because this time you're going to be mine."

Andy clicked out, but the screen turned blue, warning him not to shut off the computer. Some sort of upgrade or whatever was downloading.

He heard the front door of the house open and looked in the direction. His mom came in with a bag of groceries in one hand and her car fob in the other. "There are three more on the back seat," she said gesturing with a tilt of her chin to the one in the cruck of her arm. "Be careful," she added. "I ripped one of them trying to pick it up."

"Hello to you, too," Andy said, feigning disappointment with a well-practiced pout.

She waited for him to start past her and mid-stride leaned over to whisper a faux-kiss on his cheek. He pulled away.

"Too late to make up for it now," he said.

She knew he was just playing. "My poor baby," she said, her pout matching his. "I bought Oreos," she threw in as he went to the door, the screen door still bouncing closed.

"Now that makes it all good." There was a smile in his tone.

Outside, the porch light cast a halo along the walkway and all the way to the two-car driveway. His mom, as was her habit, parked to the far side. His dad, he knew, had always used the near side. He thought it kind of silly that his mom hadn't made the change. If only because it was that much closer.

The back door of the Jeep had been left open, and from his approach, he could see the bags upon the seat. He wondered which one had the Oreos. He'd bring that one in last so that he

40

HUNGRY

could get first dibs before Maggie stumbled upon them. He knew
she'd have come out of her room as soon as she heard mom come
in. Whatever gossip was new, she could hold it in only so long.

As Andy moved towards the door, he caught a sudden whiff of
something nasty. His first instinct was to look down to see if he
had stepped into something. There was nothing on the paved-
stone walk, and nothing on the bottom of either shoe. He checked.

Whatever it was, he thought, must have come to him on the
breeze. It was kind of dead, with only an occasional stir through
the nearby tree tops, but apparently enough to sweep along the
faint odor of the poor creature that must have lay down to die
beneath the branches, or had fallen prey to some animal which had
less of an appetite than it thought. He decided he'd go have a look
in the morning, betting it was a raccoon or possum.

At the car, he leaned in to check the bags, make sure he was
leaving the right one. As he did, he felt a strong blow to his right
hip and left butt cheek, as if he had been punched really hard in
both places at the same time. But whatever it was that hit him, had
dug into this flesh, puncturing his left cheek as if with long thorns,
and digging in too just below his ribs. It took a second more for
the pressure to turn into sharp pain. But before he could give a
second thought to his shirt and shorts being ripped away, the
sudden realization that his bareness had been exposed to the
world, he was tugged back and away from the car, and in an
instant, fully prone and face down on the oddly cool cement of the
driveway. He tried to turn and face his attacker, but as he did,
additional weight was thrown across his upper back and across the
nape of his neck. With a sudden detached panic, as if he was both
himself and someone else somewhere else, he was aware of the
flesh being torn from his backside, the teeth scraping like razors
across the bone of his hip. Then there was a sudden burn at the

41

back of his neck, a quick moment only in which so many snapshots flashed through his mind, like his father's smile, his math teacher's quirky laugh, that time he went fishing up by the pond...followed by the crunch of bone just beneath his skull.

The second creature let go of its hold at Andy's neck, aware by instinct that the prey was dead, and instead sank its teeth and elongated snout into the fleshier meat at his traps and the muscle along his shoulder. The other one, having torn away and swallowed all the flesh of Andy's buttocks, turned to the muscle at the back of his legs, the skin ripped back and sinewy tendons pulling away from the bone. Andy's lifeless body jerked with every tug.

Lisa put the bag of groceries on the kitchen table, saw the monitor on the computer across the way was black but the indicator light on, as well as the one on the tower. She smiled. What else would Andy have been doing? She turned, thinking surely, he'd be on his way back in, grocery bags in hand. Her first thought was that he had gotten distracted with something. He was just like his father when it came to that type of thing. So easily distracted.

When a handful of minutes had passed, and he had still not come through the door, she decided it was time to go check. There was milk in the one bag and chicken and burgers in the other. It wouldn't take long for any of it to go bad when it was this warm.

Opening the front door, it took a moment for her to make a connection with what she was seeing. There were two things, two figures, two man-like shapes, bent over something on the driveway. What took the moment was the realization that they were feeding, tearing away at the body on the driveway with long-fingered hands and elongated snouts, teeth gnashing and rending.

HUNGRY

With mind-numbing horror, she realized it was Andy they were tearing at. She knew, too, he was dead.

Without thinking, she rushed out the door, screaming and yelling, every intent of scaring them off. Had she been in full control of her senses at the time, she would have immediately made the connection between the smell assaulting her nostrils and what had occurred there out on the road, the animal she hit with the car. But it was the pale-yellow eyes, the large black-dot pupils which pulled her up mid-stride.

Here in the light from the porch, she saw enough of them to know they weren't bears or wolves, or any other critter she had seen in the woods, or anywhere else, for that matter. They remained crouched, back on their haunches, their long, thin arms resting on Andy's remains, his blood glinting dark red, almost black along the length of their fingers, the palm of their hands, and along the smooth, almost velvety-looking skin covering their snouts, and the lipless mouths, within which the needle-like teeth, long and cylindrical, were bared with silent snarl.

Despite her motherly instinct propelling her forward, to throw herself upon them, to get them off her son, she knew that her only chance was to get back into the house, to go for her husband's gun. But it was a realization that came too late.

Both creatures abandoned their kill at the same time, launching themselves towards her with a quickness that to Lisa seemed surreal, as is they were swimming through space. She barely had time to turn back towards the house when they were upon her. She felt the hand and long nails wrap around her left shoulder, dig in just below her collar bone as if her skin and flesh was as resistant as the surface of a puddle. The last thing she saw was the dark sky rushing away from her as she was pulled back. She never

43

HUNGRY

felt the teeth that sunk into her throat, tearing the flesh and trachea away like cotton candy. Her last breath never came.

HUNGRY

Maggie

Maggie came out of her room, an earbud plugged into one ear and her iPod in hand. She was a fan of Rock from the 80s and 90s mostly, and some of the stuff from today. In that way, she was a bit of an outcast among her friends. Among her favorites were *Iron Maiden*—she loved Bruce Dickenson, *Judas Priest*—Rob Halford's voice, she thought, was just incredible, especially on the earlier stuff, the *Scorpions*—again, it was Klaus Meine's voice, and anything with Ronnie James Dio. Well, not anything; he had a couple of real duds in there, *Angry Machines* and *Lockup the Wolves*, for instance. She also liked Bowie, some of Tull's stuff, anything with Chris Cornell, the first couple of albums by *Alice in Chains*, and you could even throw in *Planet P*. None of her friends had even heard of Tony Carey. At the moment, though, she was listening to *Catch the Rainbow*, a powerful and sometimes mellow tune by Dio when he was with *Blackmore's Rainbow*. Dio had passed away not too long ago, throat cancer, or something like that; and Bowie had died, too. Cancer, also, and just as recently. Interestingly enough, Tony Carey, the magic behind the *Planet P Project*, was the keyboard player on that album.

She smelled her mother's perfume. It wasn't strong, but just enough for Maggie to know she had come home. Coming down the hallway leading to the kitchen—most of the first floor was an open-floor plan, she expected to see her standing by the kitchen table, sipping at a tall glass of iced tea and going through the day's mail. She expected, too, to see Andy at the computer, playing his silly games. Andy and she both had their own PCs in their rooms, and both, too, had laptops. The house had Wi-Fi. Why her mother insisted on having a family computer, she didn't know. At one time it was all about internet safety, her mom's concern for strangers and the type of content kids can find when curiosity gets the better part of them. But that whole thing had faded as she and Andy went into high school, just when, Maggie thought, concerns of that type would grow—especially with a teenaged boy. She herself was neither all that curious nor all that tempted.

Not that she didn't ever, go into one of those sites, that is. Just not here at the house. The first time still filled her head with vivid imagery whenever something brought it to mind. She and Carly, her best-best friend, had a sleep over at Carly's house. Elena was there, too. It was actually Elena's idea. Not that they were being perverts, or anything like that. It started out as some giggling and silliness about the boys at school. Who had the best butt, who they thought might have the biggest thing, the smallest thing; who was doing it, and with whom? And that lead to the obvious conversation about which one of them had done what—none of them had, and who had seen what. They all had brothers. Somewhere along the line, Elena swore them to secrecy, and then said she had watched through the slightly opened door when her older brother, Emil, was doing it with his girlfriend.

"Neither one of them had a stitch of clothing on," she said, as if it would be done some other way. Then she moved in closer to them—they were all sitting on Carly's bed, queen-size—and whispered, "My brother was lying on his back and she was sitting on it, kind of bouncing up and down."

Carly had wrinkled up her nose. "And you sat there watching?"

Elena smirked. "Tell me you wouldn't."

After that, they exchanged some views on what was right and wrong when it came to privacy, and any special significance that might be attached to a sister watching a brother doing that kind of thing. Maggie thought about Andy for but a moment, and decided she couldn't imagine him with any girl bouncing on anything of his, never mind that.

Of course, it was Elena who suggested they do a search online, just kind of plugging in any word that came to mind. It wasn't long after they started that rather explicit thumbnails were popping up on the screen, and when they were clicked on, up came these short video clips. Clicking on them caused them to upload, and what happened next had all three girls exchanging looks and oh-my-Gods. By the time they had viewed the third one, and then a fourth, any need for imagination and wonder both had been expelled simultaneously, at least as far as the visual was concerned.

Not that she needed the confirmation, but the single bag of groceries sitting atop the kitchen table left no doubt that her mother was indeed home. Maggie gave a quick tug on the wire hanging from her ear and caught the descending bud in an open palm.

"Mom," she called out.

There was no answer.

Aware of the usual routine when groceries were involved, she placed the iPod and bud on the kitchen island and headed for the front door. She wanted her hands free to help with the bags.

She noted right off that the porch light was on. And too that there was a bit of a funky smell as she neared the screen, only the hint of a breeze touching her cheeks. It was an odor she couldn't immediately place, not something dead and left to bloat, and not that musky, dank stink that comes from something wet or boggy, but a smell somewhere between.

She grabbed the handle at the door, leaned down on it, and pushed open. Striding out onto the porch, she was thinking about something clever to say. But instead, her eyes fixed totally unexpectedly upon three figures crouched there beyond the porch.

47

HUNGRY

Two were but a few yards away, just off the front walkway and just outside the wash of light, and the other was there in the middle of the driveway, only a few feet from the Jeep and the rear door, which stood open. All three figures had stopped what they were doing and were staring straight up at her.

A sudden queasiness shivered her lower extremities, to the point where, unlike her mother, she did lose control and leaked upon herself. Her senses went mute. Her hearing was as if the roar of the ocean surged into her ears, and her vision telescoped, as if she had wandered into a long, dark tunnel, with only a dull light at the far end. With horror, Maggie realized that her sudden presence had distracted these things from eating, and that what they were eating was still to some degree recognizable. It all became too much, a darkness rushing up on her from someplace in her head. She swooned and then her legs turned to jelly.

As she started to drop, two things happened. The first was the realization that all three of the creatures, their eyes thin and elongated, and pale yellow with large black dots, had started for her. She wanted to scream, to give some shape to the panic which was overwhelming her. She knew she was going to die. The second was the far-off realization that a pair of hands had wrapped themselves across her breasts and that she had somehow fallen back into someone's arms.

The next thing she knew, she was thrown on to the wood floor of her living room and there was a man throwing his weight against the closed door.

Then came the realization of what she had been staring at there on the front walk and the driveway. It was her mother and brother, their bodies lifeless but recognizable from the remains which had escaped mutilation. Maggie saw the bottom of Andy's shoes, the back of his head where the hair curled up at the collar, the curve of his shoulder. She recognized her mom's scrubs, that green-colored material, particularly down around the lower legs, her brown hair, and her profile, the way her head was turned. And then, too, the bone exposed at Andy's hips, the vertebrae down the length of the spine, and no muscle, no flesh. Her mother's ribs, on her right side and all the way up to where her right arm was supposed to be, but was no more, and then all the way across her back, the spine exposed also, all the way up to the base of her skull.

"My mother, Andy," she heard herself say aloud.

The man was seated upon the floor, his back to the door, his hands pressing down at his sides, his feet set like anchors. His eyes were in line with hers. It was a face she recognized, but it was slow coming to her.

"Mr. Aloise?"

Of course, she recognized him. How would she not? Was there anyone here in the valley she wouldn't recognize, or anyone in the valley who wouldn't recognize her? He was the neighbor with the house on the other side of the hill. The neighbor whose kids were all grown, and who had all left the valley to go live elsewhere. Maggie hadn't known any of the kids all that well. She remembered the younger two, when she was but a little girl herself. But even then, they had always been more than just a few years older than she. It wasn't as if she ever played with them. It was more like she had seen them around. There were valley barbecues and block parties, things like that, back when her own father was still alive. He and Mr. Aloise were friends, neighborhood friends. She remembered Mr. Aloise coming up and over the hill, knocking on the back door once, looking to borrow a shovel or a posthole digger, something like that. But that, too, was a long time ago, back before Maggie's dad had gotten sick, or maybe just after. She couldn't remember, however, the last time she had seen him. Maybe in town, or maybe that was Mrs. Aloise. Did it matter?

"They got my Darla," she heard him say, his tone she thought remarkably flat, given the circumstances.

She wanted to get up, to go outside. It was what she'd be expected to do. But just then, the dampness against her inner thigh reminded her of her accident. And she was embarrassed, wondering what Mr. Aloise must be thinking. She put her knees together.

"Is there a gun in the house?" Mr. Aloise was asking. His hands remained pressed to the floor, his arms straight at his sides, and his weight holding against the door.

Strangely enough, Maggie saw it as an opportunity to get to her room, to get to the bathroom, to wash herself off and put on other clothes.

"In my father's closet," she said.

"Can you go get it? I don't want to move off this door."

Maggie turned away from Mr. Aloise before lifting herself from the floor. She glanced down quickly to where she had been sitting, relieved there was no puddle or sheen of wetness. Without turning, she made for the hallway.

"Make sure it's loaded," he said to her back.

When Maggie came back into the living room, she was wearing a pair of sweats with boxers beneath. She was also carrying two rifles which she had retrieved from her mother's room up on the second floor. She was tempted to look out the window while up there, but wasn't sure how she'd react seeing both her mom and brother like that, especially if those things were still feeding.

Bob saw both guns and that Maggie had changed clothing. It seemed an odd thing to do, things as they were. He gestured towards the bigger of the two guns. "Give me the Winchester," he said with a wiggle of his fingers.

Maggie handed it over to him, barrel to the ground as her father had always insisted. She had a box of ammo. It was pinched to her side beneath her elbow.

"That other one is a pop gun," Bob said with a gesture of his chin. "It'll do in a pinch, maybe to scare them off. Check to see if it's loaded."

Upon his feet, his back still against the door, Bob raised the rifle and pulled back the bolt. It wasn't loaded. He placed the box of ammo on the end table beside the couch and removed the top. He slipped in five rounds and one for the chamber. He slid the bolt home. Grabbing the gun by the barrel, he moved away from the door and positioned himself alongside the front picture window, taking care not be seen from outside the house. Extending a tentative pair of fingers, he furtively moved aside one of the slats of the vertical blinds.

From the angle he had, he couldn't see much of anything. But he was hesitant to risk putting any part of him where he might be seen. He had heard stories of bears coming right through panes of glass, and even pulling doors from the hinges. And while he knew these things, whatever they were, weren't bears, he wasn't taking any chances.

He let go of the slat he had at his fingertips, careful to keep it from swinging. He then chose another, this one further from where he stood. Again, he moved it aside ever so slightly, leaning over the arm of the couch to get a better line of sight.

It took him a second to realize he was looking at a face, an elongated snout turned in his direction and practically up against the glass. He watched as the dark lips drew back in a silent snarl. Then without warning, the snout pushed towards him. The glass held momentarily against the force, but cracked bottom to top. That's when the creature's hands came up hard, shattering the glass in shards against the blinds and falling to the couch.

Bob jumped back and at the same time brought the barrel of the gun up before him. He pulled the trigger. The shot cracked sharply, the recoil pushing back against his shoulder. Paying it no mind, he pulled back on the bolt lever ejecting the shell, and then jabbed it forward again. He fired a second time.

The blinds hanging in the way, he had no idea if either one of his shots found their target, but there was a guttural hiss and a throaty growl. The sound of falling glass upon the deck out front stopped, and so did the clatter of the slats.

Wasting no time, Bob grabbed the box of shells and turned to Maggie, who had instinctually retreated towards the kitchen.

Within two strides, Bob had her by the elbow and was pulling her towards the back door. "Go, go, go," he was barking.

Maggie wanted to protest. What sense was it running outside? That's where they were. But Mr. Aloise was so much stronger than he looked, his hands clutched around her elbow and forearm and his weight carrying her along like a wave.

Holding tight to the .22, she put up no resistance, picking up and putting down her feet to match his. Within seconds they were out the door and heading across the deck. At her back, she heard the rest of the glass in the picture window shatter and skitter across the front porch, the crash of the blinds as they, too, were pulled crashing down.

"The shed," Mr. Aloise was saying, pulling her towards the back edge of the property.

The shed was a solid wood structure without any windows and two solid doors, side-by-side. Her father had built it with his own hands. It was where they kept the ride-on lawnmower, the snow blower, and whatever other yard tools they had, shovels, rakes and whatnot.

Before Maggie realized it, she was leading the way, Mr. Aloise having pushed her out ahead of him, and he turning with every other step to see if they were being pursued. In the process, he had expelled the shell from the last shot, and had chambered another. They were not yet being pursued, but sounds coming from the house suggested at least one of the creatures had gotten inside.

Maggie reached the shed a good three or four strides before Bob did, spinning the latch that secured it closed and pulling on both handles. The doors opened without effort.

"Go in, go in," urged Mr. Aloise, coming up at her back.

Maggie did as she was told. Bob came in behind her, pulling the doors closed as he did so and shutting out any trace of the dim light coming from the back of the house.

It was pitch black, especially without any windows, and the air stifling.

"Give me a second," Bob said, reaching into his pant pocket for his lighter. He found it, and at the same time cursed himself under his breath for leaving the pack of cigarettes back at the house, his house. He could visualize them sitting there on the table next to the couch. He pulled forth the lighter and flicked his thumb across the wheel. A short flame appeared, shedding a thin halo of light between him and Maggie. It was enough to see where things were.

His eyes darting here and there, he found what he was looking for. It was an extension cord, one of those orange, industrial kind. Grabbing it, he slipped one end through the two inside door handles, back and forth in a figure-eight before tugging tightly and then tying it off. To make sure it'd hold, he pushed against the door, but only hard enough to leave himself convinced. "That should hold," he said.

Gesturing, then, to Maggie, he pointed over at the ride-on lawnmower. "May as well go and sit down. We're probably going to be here a while."

Maggie put her hand to the seat, guided herself upon it. Her mind was numb and she admonished herself, at least in thought, for thinking about her own safety while she should be doing something about her mother and brother. "Do you think they'll try to get in here?" She asked, leaning the gun against the steering wheel column, the butt on the floor.

Bob shook his head. "Not unless they track us here. Shit, how do I know? I don't even know what the fuck they are. Maybe they can smell us, maybe not." His tone, though, wasn't one of frustration or even of impatience, just of curiosity, or maybe of wonder. "There wouldn't happen to be a flashlight in here, do you think?"

Not a flashlight, Maggie didn't think. But she remembered a kerosene lamp. Her mom kept it out here because she said the kerosene smelled, and she didn't want it in the house or in the garage. She kept it out here in case the power went out, things like that. She told Mr. Aloise. "There in that cabinet. Three should be a lamp, the kind with the wick." She pointed to the back wall, above the floor.

"Good, this thing is getting hot." He was referring to the lighter.

The lamp was a smaller one with a reservoir for only two pints or so. But at least it felt full. Bob lifted off the glass tower and set the lighter to the wick. It caught immediately, a thick coil of black smoke spiraling upward. He found the little wheel and lowered the wick. The flame refined and the black smoke thinned. He placed the lamp upon the nose of the ride-on.

"We have to be quiet," he said, placing a finger long across his lips. "But at least we have some light." He then made himself a place on the floor, and sat with his back to the rear wall of the shed, facing the doors and with the rifle at the ready.

"How long do you think we'll have to be in here?" Maggie whispered.

Bob hadn't given it any thought. "Maybe sunrise," he said. Then: "We probably shouldn't talk."

It wasn't that much later that they heard snuffling not too far from the shed, and then a sort of snorting, or some other throaty sound. It may have been those things communicating, and maybe not. Either way, it didn't come any closer, and not much later—though it seemed much longer, it was gone.

At one point, Mr. Aloise suggested Maggie try and get some sleep. She leaned forward and put her head in her arms across the steering wheel of the ride-on, but whenever she closed her eyes, her head filled with images of Andy lying face down on the driveway and her armless mom. She felt the tears rolling down her cheeks, but couldn't find the voice to cry.

Bob, eventually feeling safe enough to follow his own advice, let his eyes close. He fell asleep thinking on his cigarettes.

HUNGRY

Sheriff Hardy

Heading up Sylvan Road, Sheriff Hardy was glad to see that Guy had opened up early this morning. He looked down at the clock on the dashboard of the Chrysler *300*. It was 7:48. Normally, at this time the sun would be just coming up over the trees at the top of the hill and he would have the sun visor down and tilted to shade the glare. But not today. The clouds were thick and grey, and the humidity already near unbearable. He had the window up and the AC on high. No doubt they were in store for some rain. He pressed his finger to the radio icon to listen to the weather report. But even with the car's technology, there wasn't much that could be done about the reception down in the valley. He ignored the crackling as he made the right into the parking lot. It was the coffee he was after.

Guy was in the store by himself, sweeping the floor by the refrigerated cases at the back. He was a big man, wide at the shoulders and with a pronounced belly providing evidence of his love of beer. He was also probably the only one in the valley who still wore his hair in his interpretation of the traditional Native American style: pulled back behind the ears and braided tightly like a rope long down the middle of his back. Off-hand, he couldn't think of anyone in the valley without Mohawk lineage, even though Alba had married Mexican. Nevertheless, the whole valley belonged to the tribe and was legally reservation land—a sovereign nation. It's just that no one felt the need to go up into the hills and shout it out on a routine basis.

Sheriff Hardy himself was pure-blood, with the three generations proceeding him all born here in the valley, living their whole lives in the valley, and most buried back up in the hills in

56

the cemetery. His mom and dad, both well into their eighties, were still alive and in the same house in which he grew up. Back up the hills, way over on the other side of their property, still to this day, there were the sacred burial grounds. But no one, other than teenagers seeking a ghostly thrill, went out that way. Not that it was taboo, but that, well, death back then wasn't quite seen the same way. You didn't mention the name of the dead, other than ritually, and even then, only if you were family. There wasn't much thought given to what came after. It was all different plane stuff. The dead simply went back to where they came from in the first place. Wherever that was.

These days, what with just about everyone in the valley being Christian and attending the local church, a proper service was the way to go, and burials were all prim and proper. The church itself went back to just after the Revolutionary War. It was built by missionaries who, as the story goes, seeking shelter during a particularly rough stretch of winter, stumbled upon a small band of Mohawks, who themselves fleeing from the colonial militia pursuing the British north towards Canada and slaughtering native tribes along the way, sought refuge down the other side of the steep hills among the dense trees which lined the valley. Some chose to stay, while the greater part of their people eventually settled in territory bordering Ontario, and which remains today the largest Mohawk reservation in the north. Either the, missionaries, too, chose the valley.

Sheriff Hardy remembered his great-grandfather telling him stories when Hardy was only a boy, the old man's voice quiet but rich, and the words coming slow. It was he who told him of the original settlers—his grandfather was one, if only a boy at the time himself—and their every intention of rejoining the others. But come that first spring, the valley was so rich in natural resources,

HuNGRY

and so wonderfully secluded, that the decision was made to stay. The fight to have the valley recognized as reservation land dragged on for multiple generations, before finally being federally established in 1967, and even then, as a part of the already recognized Mohawk lands up north, and initially, at least, subject to the dictates of the larger tribal council. Apparently, there was a precedence established in other states, but particularly Utah and Nevada. Since then, however, owing mainly to the distance separating the two, the valley had developed its own independence, meeting with the larger council only on matters which required nothing less.

Unlike many reservations, the community choose not to make a big deal out of the notion of sovereignty, and though benefitting to some degree from the status, preferred to integrate themselves within the neighboring communities and practice the more general values of society. There was, for example, no smoke shops or interest in a casino. Education, too, was highly valued, incomes were generally above the norm, and most of the community held professional positions either here in the valley or in the outside world, including the Sheriff's own son.

Sovereignty, though, wasn't without its challenges, one of which was the smallness of the police force. Besides Sheriff Hardy, there were five deputies, two fulltime receptionists, one part-time receptionist, and the whole valley to cover. Basically, they ran three two-man shifts, with no receptionist from 11 pm to 7 am, except on Friday and Saturdays. Experience had taught the Sheriff that those two nights were generally longer than the other days of the week. One of his receptionists was his wife of 42 years; they were both 63. One was his only daughter, the middle child of three. She was married to one of his deputies; nine years it was now. They had two children of their own: his grandson, recently turned seven, and his granddaughter, age five. One of his two sons, the youngest, was also a deputy. Like his older brother, he had at one time moved out of the valley and was working as a State Trooper. He gave it up after four years, and at age 29 he accepted his father's offer, and came back to take the place of Big Red Harrison, who decided that, at age 70, it was time to retire. Sheriff Hardy's oldest son was a professor of anthropology at a big city university. They saw each other mainly on the holidays.

Guy looked up from his broom as the bell above the door rang. Noticing the Sheriff, he pointed to the pot of coffee behind the counter. "Help yourself, Harvey. It just brewed fresh."

The Sheriff nodded his appreciation and detoured to the other side of the cash register. "Wasn't sure you'd be open this early."

Guy shrugged, pulled a small pile of dust and loose papers towards him, a dustpan at his feet. "Didn't sleep well last night. Tossed and turned. Saw no sense in staying in bed, so I got up, made myself some breakfast, and decided to come into the store, do so straightening before we get busy."

Hardy pulled the large-sized Styrofoam cup from the stack, poured himself a small pyramid of sugar at the bottom, and then filled the cup to the brim. No milk. He liked it black and sweet. Whenever someone would make comment, he was known to say that if milk was what he wanted, it was milk he'd drink.

"You haven't noticed anything strange or different going on out this way?" He asked.

Guy lowered himself with one knee not quite touching the floor, retrieved the dustpan. "What do you have in mind?"

Hardy shrugged, then took a moment to sip from the rim of the cup. The coffee was hot, almost too hot to taste. He blew gently across the surface. Tried again. Better, he thought. "Not sure. I'm on my way out to the Steed place. Seems the Torres boy stumbled across something. He came home and told his ma, and she called it in."

Guy was expecting Joseph Torres to come in to work at nine. "Wasn't Joseph, was it?"

Hardy shook his head, took another sip, this one deeper and longer. The caffeine was already starting to do its thing. "I believe she said it was Peter."

Guy looked relieved. "Good. It wouldn't do me any good if the boy was to be delayed. He's a good worker." He let his eyes circle the store. "There's a lot that needs to be done this morning."

Hardy nodded in agreement, though he thought the place looked as well-kept as always.

"So, anyways, what was it the boy stumbled across?"

Hardy thought a moment before answering. Decided he might as well go ahead and say. "Something may have happened to Barry Steed. Alba seemed kind of flustered, if you know what I mean. Said something about bones and blood in the grass. She said the boy was talking about what looked like clothing. I could hear his voice in the background. He did sound rattled. Anyway, I'm going out to have a look."

Guy's lips were pressed together. "No, I haven't seen or heard nothing like that around here, no coyotes or bears, if that's what you're asking. I hate to think of it, but could be a cat—mountain lion. It's not unheard of, as you know."

Hardy popped a lid across the top of the cup, peeled back the tab. It stuck in the little slot tight on the first try. "Well, I better be getting out there. I left a dollar by the register." He gestured with tip of his head.

"Let me know what you find out. I'd hate to think something bad has happened to Barry."

Hardy didn't seem all that concerned. "Probably just a coon."

HUNGRY

Sheriff Hardy thought about making the turn at the lane leading to the Torres' house, but decided against it. Instead, he kept to Sylvan and directly to the Steed place. In his experience, kids tended to play things up a bit, exaggerate what they see. It would be better, he thought, just to go and see for himself, then if necessary, talk to the boy afterwards.

The Steed property was off the south side of the road, down a narrow dirt lane and up the rise. He made a mental note to see if the lane was on the latest list of roads to be paved. Still quite a few of the smaller ones up this way that needed to be done, though no one was complaining. The house sat deep back in the property, out of sight and back beyond the thick cover of tall trees which grew out front. The hill to the back of the house was one of the steeper climbs in the valley and with no let-up of trees. As for the house itself, it was a two-story structure with a doghouse roof, a second story porch out back, and a couple of dormers, one to each side, added later on. There was a deep garage up at the end of the drive and connected to the house by a covered run.

As for Hardy, he hadn't been out to see Barry Steed since his wife, Mary, had passed. Barry kind of kept to himself before her passing, and nothing changed following. People in the valley found him to be both a bit obnoxious and a bit arrogant, but Hardy thought him a likeable guy despite the fact. Of course, part of it was that they had gone to school together and pretty much grew up together, even if Barry was three years older. Hardy remembered him as a pretty good baseball player that had an arm that if things had gone his way could have taken him big time. It was cliché, Hardy knew, but something went wrong with Barry's shoulder the summer before his senior year, and things were never the same after that. It was a summer game over in West Gate

61

against a bunch of white kids. Right there in the middle of an inning, Barry reached for the back of his left shoulder. Hardy was playing second base. The coach came out right after that, and after a brief discussion, the two of them walked off together. Before they got back to the bench area, Barry had already flung his glove over the low, flat roof above the bench, and as far as Hardy knew, that was the last time he played.

As did Hardy, Barry went to the community college, spent his two years, and then took a job with a manufacturer on the north side of the city. As far as Hardy knew, he stayed with that company for forty years before retiring only a year or two ago. He had no idea if that retirement came with a pension, but Barry never seemed to want for anything. He also made it a routine to stop in every Friday night at the Bent Arrow for a beer and a shot, and also on Sunday afternoons for the same. He was a big New York Mets fan, and loved to watch the Jets and Knicks, also. Never seemed to lack for conversation when he was there. That he always bought a round probably didn't hurt any.

Alba Torres had mentioned the garage. It was over by the garage that Peter saw what he saw, that's what she had said. How old was that kid now? Hardy asked himself. Twelve, maybe thirteen. Whichever, it was an age where he would know pretty much what he was looking at. Coming across partially or even fully eaten carcasses, bone and hide or fur piled about, was a fairly common sight in these parts. There were small varmints behind just about every tree, and coyotes, especially, had become an ever-increasing nuisance. Three or four of those things could easily take down a doe or smallish deer with no trouble at all. They'd eat their fill and leave the rest for the scavengers. Surely, though, a boy Peter's age, twelve or thirteen, would know a deer carcass when he saw one. And having seen one, he wouldn't be running home to tell his ma to call the sheriff.

Hardy turned the car up the drive, the loose blue-stone crackling beneath the tires, and the house came into view. Barry's truck wasn't in the driveway. Probably in the garage, was Hardy's first thought. He doubted Barry was up and around this early in the morning. He pulled the *300* up towards the house, turned off the engine, and got out. As soon as he did, he got a good look right away at what it was that must have caught the Torres kid's eye. There were glinting ribbons streaked across the tops of the tall grass, as if someone were using a brush to flick paint across a canvas, unconcerned as to just where that paint might land or what it might look like. The way the daylight caught it, he couldn't tell with any certainty what color it might be, but, too, he saw what looked to be a few indistinguishable clumps here and there, and not too far one from the other. He actually paused a moment, considering whether he should go knock on the door first or take a closer look. At least, he thought, if Barry answered, he'd be less put off by what he might find.

But his curiosity won out. He stepped across the driveway and onto the grass. Before he had cause to go any further, it became quite apparent that the streaks were dark red, and undoubtedly blood. More disconcerting yet were the obvious strips and swatches of clothing which gave shape and form to the clumps he was seeing. He edged closer and bent to take a better look. There was no need for a second glance to know he wasn't looking at a deer, or a raccoon, or even a coyote. Not unless the local fauna had taken to wearing colored t-shirts lately.

Hardy saw that the seam that made up the V-neck of the navy-blue t-shirt was still intact. However, above it there was no head. Below, there was no substantial cloth, only shredded remains which had fallen off to either side of where the torso had at one time been. Now, there was only a partial rib cage, the ribs remaining stripped clean of any flesh, gouged and licked down to the white of the bone. All of the organs, too, were gone, and the spine—fully revealed—was beneath the rib cage and lying flat to the grass. Here and there, and still attached to the occasional vertebrae, were thin patches of skin, pale and erose around the edges. There were no legs and no arms, and a lot less blood on the ground, especially there were the remains lay, than Hardy would have thought. A quick glance gave him a good idea as to where the limbs had gone, maybe the head, too. He cringed with the realization that the Torres boy had probably been standing in this same spot and looking at the same mess.

Hardy had little doubt he was looking at the remains of poor Barry. And no way, he thought, was he the victim of a bear attack. Too much scattering of the remains. Perhaps a pack of coyotes could have made this kind of mess, pulling parts off to themselves. But then again, he didn't think coyotes were strong enough to pull away the arms and legs like Barry's seemed to have been. Not the ones in these hills. Maybe a mountain lion, then, a big male. But then again, a big cat wouldn't account for, well, the scattering of the remains.

It wasn't until he turned with the intent to head towards the front door of the house, however, that his eye caught the glint of something that didn't look like streaks of blood. He took a step closer, mindful of not imposing himself any more than necessary on the crime scene. There just to the far side of the body and lying in a way that he hadn't at first noticed was Barry's shotgun. Hardy nodded. That was enough to suggest some kind of animal, he decided. Had to be if Barry came out here with gun in hand. But

he told himself, that didn't necessarily mean it was that animal that
did this.

As Hardy had expected, unfortunately, neither the screen door nor
the main door of the house was locked, the main door pretty much
wide open. Hardy didn't bother to knock. He went right in, calling
out to Barry. He didn't anticipate a response, but he could always
hope. It was possible that the remains out on the lawn belonged to
someone else. He found the TV on, but not the volume, further
indication that Barry had heard something out in the yard, muted
the sound on the set so he could be sure, and then went out to
chase away whatever it was. There was a mug of beer, half-filled,
sitting on the end table. It was warm and flat. The lamp was still
on.

He made a cursory search of the house, more so sticking to
protocol than anything else. Nothing looked disturbed; he was
impressed by how neatly the house had been kept, assuming that
things would have been lacking in that department since Mary had
passed. But no: the beds were made—even in the unused
bedrooms; there weren't any pots or pans in the sink; the stovetop
was clear; there wasn't even any dust on any of the surfaces,
something he couldn't say about his own house.

He made sure to lock and fully close the door as he went out,
checking first that he had taken the right key off the hook in the
kitchen. He'd have whoever it was on duty this morning come out
to the house, take photos, wait for Dr. Dave, and basically process
the whole scene.

Back in the car, he made a call into the station. It was Tanya
who took the call. "Who's on duty this morning?" He asked.

"That'd be Jeremy," she answered.

"Is he there yet?"

"Just walked in."

Hardy looked down at the time. It was a few minutes after eight. "Tell him I need him out at the Steed house. And I need you to get a call into Dr. Dave or Dr. Lisa. Tell whichever to put his or her coroner's hat on. We got a body…or at least, what's left to it."

"Barry Steed?" Tanya did nothing to hide her concern or surprise.

"Looks that way."

"Heart attack?"

"Not that I could tell."

"10-4. What's your 20?"

"Right now, I'm in the Steed driveway, but I'm on my way over to the Torres' place. Tell Jeremy to call me when he gets out here. I put the key to the front door beneath the mat. Tell him to process the inside of the house, also. The crime scene is to the left of the driveway, out by the garage. He'll see it."

"You got it, chief. Over."

"Over," Hardy repeated.

He was barely down at the end of the driveway when the radio crackled and Tanya was coming back at him, her voice pitched with emotion and clearly shaken.

"There's been a horrible accident over at Dr. Lisa's place. She and the boy, Andy, are dead. I've got her daughter, Maggie, on the phone."

Hardy backed the car onto the road, headed out towards Sylvan. "I'm on my way, over."

HUNGRY

Blood inside the House

Bob didn't think there was any way in the world that he was going to fall asleep. Not after all of this. He even promised himself that he'd stay awake, keep guard, gun across his lap, and make sure nothing came through those shed doors. And even though he encouraged Maggie to try and get some sleep, after what she had seen, he was surprised when he looked over and saw her chest rising and falling slowly and rhythmically. He was tempted to call over to her, ask her if she was sleeping. But he didn't.

It must have been shortly after that that he too nodded off, because that's the last thing he remembered. In fact, if he hadn't just awakened, he wouldn't have realized he had fallen asleep in the first place. No dreams, no nothing. Out like a light.

And it was the light squeezing in at the bottom of the doors that told him that they'd made it through the night. Other than that little bit, though, the inside of the shed was still dark, the kerosene lamp having burned through what fuel there was while they slept. There was the odor of it in the air and a lingering tingle at the tip of his tongue.

Remembering his lighter, he dug it out of his pocket and gave it a flick. The flame was there immediately, providing enough light for him to see Maggie. Her head was nestled in her arms, her arms crossed atop the steering wheel of the ride-on mower. She stirred just then.

Bob wasn't sure if he should say something, wake her up, or just let her be. But what he really wanted to do was to go to those doors, put his ear up against them, and hear if there was anything to hear.

Maggie muttered something in her sleep.

67

HUNGRY

Bob didn't quite catch it. Gently he reached over and placed his hand on her shoulder. Gave her the slightest nudge while saying her name softly.

Maggie's head came up from her arms but a couple of inches. Turned away from Bob, she remained still, obviously disoriented.

Bob gave her a moment or two before he nudged her again, gently, and said her name.

Maggie turned her head towards her name, pushing up slowly from the steering wheel, but not all the way and her hands still holding tight. It took her another moment before she fully realized where she was. And then the horror of the previous night came flooding back to her. She snapped full-up with a start, banging both her knees beneath the steering wheel and almost falling back off the seat.

Bob caught her, kept her from going over. "It's okay. We're safe. We're fine." He knew it wasn't the proper thing to say, the girl losing her mother and brother like that, but it's what came out.

The cigarette lighter providing so little in the way of light, he was glad he couldn't see her face too well, the helplessness and emptiness she must be feeling, or she his. He had his own wife to think of, but it was nowhere near the same, a grown man like him and a little girl like her.

"Sit here," he said. "I'm going to go over by the door, take a look."

He thought she'd say something, perhaps tell him not to. But she didn't. The pale light playing off her eyes with a greenish glint, first she looked up at him and then turned her head slowly towards the doors.

He checked the safety on the rifle. It was off. He then steadied it with his right hand, finger poised before the trigger and barrel raised. With his left hand he fumbled away the extension cord,

68

then ever so quietly pushed on the handles, the ear he considered his good one turned but slightly. He heard nothing to keep him from opening the two doors wide. Standing centered in the frame, he took in a landscape view. The sky was overcast and gray atop the trees ringing the yard. The lawn, green and well-manicured, glistened with the early morning dew like tiny globes hinting of rainbows. Other than that, the house was quiet and there was nothing to worry his attention. He stepped out onto the ramp.

Before moving down the shallow slope, Bob signaled Maggie to stay where she was but didn't look back to see if she saw. At the bottom of the ramp, he took in the whole of the backyard, saw what he could around each side of the house. Over the roof, he noted the tops of the trees that ran up the hill across the way, a dark green staircase into the pale red sky. The sun was hidden behind a ruffled blanket of morning clouds. There was a slight breeze which, despite the early hour, pushed the heavy, humid air into his face. Of the creatures, however, there was no sign.

"It's safe, Maggie. Come on. Let's get back into the house." This time he turned to see if she was with him, the corner of his eye kept to the yard.

Maggie was there at the doors, stopped short of coming out. She had the .22 in her hand, but it was drooping towards the ground. Bob thought about saying something, let it go. Her eyes were looking all about, warily, but not fear-filled.

"It's okay," said Bob. "They're gone."

Maggie made her way down the ramp. Eyes darting about, she first scanned the tree lines on each side of the yard, then traced the path to the back deck, picturing herself crossing it, too, and then safely within the house. But then she remembered the glass of the picture-window, first cracking and then falling in, the sound of it breaking upon the porch and clattering down the vertical blinds.

HUNGRY

Worse than that, though, and the possibility one of those things, or all of them, might still be in the house, was her mother and brother out in the front yard. There was no way she was going to be able to deal with that, and no way, too, she was going to be able to go back into the house and then not look.

Mr. Aloise came to her then, taking her by the hand. His grip was gentle, but firm. It was a father's grip, not much different than her own dad. Together they covered the distance from the shed to the deck. Maybe for the first time, Maggie realized just how expansive a yard it was, walking quickly as they were and seemingly with each stride covering so little ground.

And then they were through the back door and into the kitchen.

The first thing Maggie saw was her phone, there atop the island where she had left it. Mr. Aloise saw it, too. "Where's the house phone?" He asked. She pointed to the nook the other side of the refrigerator.

Bob moved towards the phone, but then decided he better check out the rest of the house before doing anything else. At this point, their immediate situation was more important than making a call to the sheriff, which wasn't going to change anything that had already happened.

He made his way first over towards the smashed picture window. The top balance for the vertical blinds had been pulled from the wall. It lay partially across the top of the couch and partially out through the open space where the pane used to be. Much of the broken glass had fallen to the couch, some across the coffee table, and some upon the floor. The front door remained closed. He noticed, too, a dark substance staining the edge of the couch, and more of it too on the floor. It was then that he realized he had tracked through some of it, and whatever it was, he was

70

leaving faint imprints in his wake where it had gotten on the bottom of his shoe. If he had to guess, he'd say it was blood from that thing. One of his shots, at least, must have hit home. Other than that, though, there were no other signs of the critters. He refrained from actually standing out in the open and looking out at the front lawn and the driveway. The priority, he decided, was to make sure the rest of the house was clear.

He turned back to where Maggie was in the kitchen and told her to remain put. "I'm going to check the rest of the house. Keep that gun at the ready."

He made his way through the rest of the first floor, taking a quick look at both Maggie's and Andy's bedrooms. He was surprised both at how big they were—both larger than the master back in his own house, and how well-apportioned. Both had queen-size beds, large flat-screen televisions, very nice audio equipment, walk-in closets, on-suite bathrooms—even he didn't have that, and all kinds of dressers and desk space. He was impressed. I guess even small-town doctors make pretty good money, he said to himself, after which he immediately admonished himself for being insensitive given the latest events. Poor kid, he thought.

He left both rooms behind, satisfied there was nothing there, and then searched what appeared to be a family or TV room. There was nothing to indicate any critter was there at any time. He headed back to the kitchen, poking his head in to ask Maggie if she was alright before going up the stairs. She nodded in response, her iPhone in hand. She didn't say anything.

Bob immediately noticed the small dots of dark substance on the stairs. They appeared on every other one, top to bottom, and then again on the second-floor landing. He brought the rifle up at the ready.

HUNGRY

There were two rooms on the second floor: the master and what appeared to be a professional home office, filled with book-lined shelves along three of the four walls, a large desk besides which was another system of shelving housing a real fancy computer, printer, scanner, and modem. The key board and the biggest monitor Bob had ever seen were on the desk. He didn't see any wires. He noticed, too, spots of blood—that's what he was calling it—on the floor, but only a few strides into the room. The same was true of the master. It was obvious that at least one of the creatures, one of those things—the one he shot, had come this far, didn't find what it was looking for, and left.

He went back downstairs, satisfied they were safe. There was nothing in the house to be afraid of.

Lifting the phone from the cradle, he used the landline to call the sheriff's office. 911 was 911, even here in the valley.

Sheriff Hardy was playing over in his head the conversation he had with Tanya. She told him that it was Bob Aloise who called, and he called from Dr. Lisa's house. According to what Aloise told her, Dr. Lisa and her son Andy were both attacked and killed by some sort of animals—more than one, their bodies, or at least what remained of them, still lying out on the front lawn and driveway, for all he knew. He told Tanya he wasn't going out to check, that he and Maggie, Dr. Lisa's daughter, were holed up in the house after spending the night out in the shed.

Hardy asked Tanya to clarify what Aloise meant by some kind of animal. She said that Aloise wasn't clear on the matter, saying only that he didn't get a real good look at them, but from what he did see, they didn't look like anything he had ever seen before.

HUNGRY

"He mentioned the eyes," she emphasized to Hardy, "more than once. He described them as elongated, Asian-like, with large black pupils."

"Eyes? That's all he saw?"

"Eyes, that's what he talked about. He said he got a look at it in his own yard. Apparently, the same animals, or whatever they were, attacked his wife Darla."

Hardy asked Tanya to repeat what she just said. After she did, he said, "And when were you going to tell me that?" He also got from her that *attacked* meant *killed*.

"Sorry," she apologized. "I thought I told you."

The Aloise house, he knew, was down the other side of the hill. He couldn't see Bob Aloise running all that distance, especially uphill.

Tanya went on to tell Hardy that Aloise said the things were upright and like no wild creature he had ever seen before, not here in these woods or in the surrounding hills, or even anything he'd seen on television or on Nat-Geo.

"He said Nat-Geo?" Hardy asked.

Tanya laughed when she repeated it, not meaning to do so. She covered the insensitivity with a quick cough. "That's what he said. He also said that they were the same critters that got Dr. Lisa and the boy. Maggie saw them, too."

Tanya had said something else right after that, but Hardy's thoughts were elsewhere. He didn't ask what it was, and instead asked if Jeremy was on his way over to the Steed place and did Tanya get in touch with Dr. Dave?

Tanya answered affirmative to both.

He knew the doctor's house was coming up, so he told her he'd check back shortly, ended by telling her to tell Jeremy what she had told him and that he ought to be extra careful.

HUNGRY

Dr. White dead. The sheriff let the thought take shape, wanted to reject it. He'd known Dr. Lisa White from the moment of her birth. Was there when she buried her husband Michael. Cursed the cancer that took him and left those two children fatherless.

Hardy came around the curve in the road, passed the trees down the side of the property, saw the long front yard, the driveway to his right. His attention was pulled immediately to the open door of the black Cherokee parked in the driveway up close to the garage. The upward slope of the drive gave him an unobstructed view of the stain there on the ground, just beyond the open door, and something else, which from this distance he couldn't make out with any clarity. He let his eyes move towards the lawn, going on what Tanya had told him. There was something there, too. His heart sank.

He pulled the *300* up the apron of the drive, brought the car to a stop well before the back of the Jeep. He pushed the ignition button to shut off the engine, then opened the door and stepped out into the warm, humid air. Looking over to the house, he saw first the broken glass of the picture window, long, sharp shards of glass hanging down like fangs from the upper part of the sash, stabbing up from the lower one. He then saw the blood on the driveway and what were clearly human remains. He saw, too, something similar just this side of the front walkway and on the grass. He took a deep slow breath and started around the front of the car.

The remains beside the Cherokee were limited to the spinal column collapsed towards the surface of the driveway and lying atop what was left of the rib cage. Most of the ribs seemed to be accounted for, and there was a long, thin patch of skin, pale and torn around the edges. The head was gone, as were the arms.

74

HUNGRY

There were no organs from what Hardy could tell. Both pelvis bones were visible, devoid of any flesh, and scarred with teeth marks. Hardy had seen something similar—teeth to bone—with animal kills. Both femur bones had been pulled away from the hips, one lying to one side of the body, and the other to the other. They, too, had been cleaned of any flesh and muscle. The lower legs were there, too, and mainly recognizable due to the sneakered feet which were still intact, the flesh at the base of the tibia gnawed away, and the socks bloodied. A few feet away, closer to the edge of the driveway nearest to the house, was some cloth, the pattern and material of which suggested what was left of a pair of shorts and some boxers. Nearer to the body was the shredded remains of what most likely was the shirt Andy was wearing. Hardy noted professionally the similarities to the scene at the Steed place, and then he hoped that it was over quickly, finding no way to imagine the sheer terror and panic the boy must have been going through.

Within the few, short strides it took him to get over to Dr. Lisa, Hardy had found that place mentally and emotionally for which he was well-known. It was the ability to cocoon himself away from feelings, to find an eye of calm in the middle of chaos and confusion. His wife called it de-empathizing, and she meant it in a positive way. It was his way of compartmentalizing the feelings he had for others, those close to him, like friends and family, as well as those he served, putting them off to the side for the moment at-hand, and by doing so, allowing himself to see the moment objectively. It was, he knew, what made him so damned good at his job.

What he found with Dr. Lisa wasn't all that different than what had been done with Andy. The head was gone. Both arms were gone. There was nothing he recognized as looking like a humerus, radius or ulna. He could see what looked like the scapula, attached though partially fractured, and also the clavicle, parts of which looked to have been gnawed away. The legs, he thought, probably had been dismembered simultaneously, probably with one or two forceful tugs. The green scrubs she was wearing as pants were seemingly fully intact, a few feet down the lawn, and with deep blood stains along the waistband. The skeletal remains of both legs were still intact, with the tibia and fibula still attached to the femur at the knee joint. Her feet, too, just like Andy's, still filled her white sneakers, dark blood soaked into the socks.

As Hardy bent over the remains, getting a closer look at obvious teeth marks to the bones, he heard the front door of the house open. Turning, he saw Bob Aloise coming across the porch, rifle in hand, and doing his best to sidestep pieces of broken glass. His first thought was for Maggie.

"Where's the girl?" He asked.

Bob nodded towards the house. "She's inside."

"Good. I don't want her seeing this."

Bob came down the stairs. Moving in the sheriff's direction, he came only a step onto the lawn before stopping. Unprepared for what he saw, he turned away, swallowing hard against the ball in his throat. "I guess I didn't expect to see that," he said.

"I'm sorry. I would have warned you if I knew you were there. It's best you not walk around here, anyway. Best not to disturb anything until we can do an official investigation. Why don't you go back in the house? I'll put a call into Tanya, and I'll be right in. Oh, and Bob, don't let Maggie come out here."

Bob was already on his way back up the stairs. "No, I won't."

HUNGRY

Back to Bob's house

Sheriff Hardy had just come back into Dr. Lisa's house, joining Bob Aloise at the kitchen table. They had been waiting for Carly's mother to come and pick up Maggie, take her back to their house. Both he and Aloise were amazed by Maggie, talking to Carly on her iPhone and explaining the situation calmly and in control, the same as they had rehearsed it.

"It's best," Sheriff Hardy had told her, "if you tell Carly that there was an accident and ask her if it would be okay for you to stay with her a while. Have her mother come and pick you up. If it's not a problem, tell her to put her mom on the phone, and then let me speak to her."

Hardy took the phone when the moment came and walked down the hallway so that he wouldn't be heard. He explained to Monica, Carly's mother, only as much as he felt was necessary. He did tell her that both Lisa and Andy were involved in a serious accident, and that he'd prefer, actually insisted, that Monica should come only as far as the curve on Sylvan, and not up to the house. He promised he'd explain later, and that, he was sure, Maggie would probably want to talk, too. "Call me when you get to the curve, and I'll bring Maggie over to you." He gave her his own cell number.

To get Maggie out to the car, he covered her head with a towel he found in the bathroom and made her promise not to look. "I'm going to lead you down the lawn and into the road. And I don't want you to see what's out there."

Maggie did as she was told, making sure to squeeze her eyes tightly shut the whole while she felt grass underfoot. Sheriff Hardy made her stay beneath the towel until they were beyond the trees, and then slid it off, telling her not to look back.

Once they were at the car, Hardy beckoned Monica to come out while Maggie got into the back seat with Carly. Keeping his voice down, he informed Monica that both Lisa and Andy had been killed, but that he wasn't able to give her details at the time, other than to say it looked like an animal attack of some sort.

"Maggie saw part of the attack," he told her.

Monica was horrified. She then assured him that Maggie could stay with her family for as long as needed.

Hardy assured her he'd make arrangements for Maggie to get her things, and see, too, if he could track down the school social worker and psychologist. He then stood there at the side of the road while Monica did a three-point turn and went back the way she came. He could see, too, that she was turning her head as if saying something to either Carly or Maggie or both. Maggie and Carly were sitting side-by-side and Maggie's head was down.

Hardy waited for the car to get out of sight. He then returned to the house where Bob was waiting.

The two of them sitting at the kitchen table, Bob still holding tight to the rifle, Hardy said, "If you're up to it, Bob, I think we better go have a look at your place. My deputies are on the way to take over here. They'll do the proper thing by Dr. Lisa and Andy. But listen, I understand if you prefer to stay here. I can go by myself."

Bob shook his head. "No, I'll go with you. She's my wife, after all, and for all I know Ruff's running loose out there, too."

It took Hardy a moment to realize Bob was talking about his dog. "Good. Let's give it a few minutes for my guys to get here, and then we'll go."

Bob nodded.

HUNGRY

Hardy took a breath and let a moment pass. "Can you tell me what you saw? Both at your place and here."

Bob shrugged. "Can't say I actually *saw* all that much." He then told Hardy about Darla giving him shit about the dog; she catching an attitude; he hearing the back door opening, the dog running out, some barking, and then Darla scream. "That got me moving," he said with a short chuckle. "You know how she gets. I'm thinking, she's yelling at the dog. But then she lets out a second holler, and this one's for real, one of those terror screams.

"Well, I went out running, and I don't see her out there in back of the house, and Ruff is gone, too. I don't know what made me do it, but I went towards the far side of the house, towards where the trail goes up the hill. That's when I saw two of them, crouched down near to the ground and having a go at something. I had no idea just then what I was looking at. But then, first one and then the other kind of turned and looked up at me. All I saw, really, were those yellow eyes, kind of long and turned-up like a china man, and with big black pupils like dead center. And there was this smell, almost as bad as some dead thing decaying.

"I don't mind telling you, I almost pissed myself right there. My legs went wobbly, but my brain was screaming run. I don't know why, but I never even thought about trying to get back to the house. I just started up the hill, and that's when I caught sight of another one coming across my backyard and right at me. I have no idea how I got away." He shrugged. "Maybe they decided I wasn't worth the chase just then."

Hardy thought he'd push a little. "You must have seen more than just the eyes. Something that told you it wasn't bears, or coyotes, or even a mountain lion."

"Fuck, Harvey. It was pitch black out there. You know how it gets. The only light was what was coming from the windows of my house, and that wasn't worth a shit. Even here at Doc's house, when I shot at the things, it was the other side of the blinds. The only thing I could tell you for certain is that they were upright, or at least that's how they moved, going by the one that was coming at me in my yard and the one trying to come through the window."

Hardy leaned back in the chair, taking the two front legs off the floor. "See? Now that's something. So, they move upright. Would you say from what you saw that they were as big as a man? You know, like you and me? Had legs like a man? Arms like a man? Or would you definitely say animal-like?"

Aloise knew what Hardy was getting at. "Let me see," he said while trying to collect his thoughts, think back upon what he might have seen. "Man, it was dark, and they were crouched. But if I had to guess, I'd say somewhat smaller, not as tall and not as big." He rounded and extended both hands out in front of him. "And kind of like a dog's face, with the snout, I mean. But not as pronounced, not as long."

"Like a pug, or something similar?" Hardy suggested.

Aloise shook his head. "No, nothing like that, not pushed in or pushed back. Definitely extended, just not as long. And it didn't seem to have lips, not the one I saw up close by the window, not pronounced, anyway. Thin. Black, maybe not. Its teeth were exposed, as if it was snarling. I wish I could tell you what color, but other than the face, the rest of it just seemed to blend with the dark." He then said, "Those spots on the floor there in the living room, on the couch, and up the stairs, too, I'm pretty sure its blood from the one I shot."

"So you said." Hardy had already given them the once over. He couldn't say if it was blood, though. He put the tip of his index finger to one of the larger spots, found the substance to be both tacky to the touch and somewhat viscous, much like oil—it even had a bit of surface sheen. "I'll make sure the guys get a sample. Let Dr. Dave take a look at it, see what he can tell us."

The deputies arrived moments later, the SUV pulling up down beside the driveway and the sound of two doors left to close with a push.

"You're okay to go out there, right?" Hardy asked as he got himself up out of the chair.

Bob kept his response to a nod.

Once outside the house, Bob, at Hardy's insistence, went straight to the *300*, taking the passenger seat up front, pulling the door closed, and glad there was a tint to the windows. Despite the car having sat for a good thirty minutes or so, there was still a touch of coolness, but the air was noticeably closed and somewhat stifling, nonetheless.

Hardy went over to greet his two deputies, one of whom was his son David. The other was a rookie by the name of Eric Swan. He, too, had grown up in the valley, and had only recently received his associate degree from the community college. For all intents and purposes, he was still probationary and still in training. Hardy took a look at his boyish face, and thought for a moment that he probably should have had Tanya send someone else.

"I want to give you both a head's up," he said. "It's not pretty."

While Hardy walked the other two through the crime scene, pointing out what he felt he needed to point out, and making sure they knew what to do and how to do it, Bob remained in the car with the door closed, despite the lack of air and the growing oppressiveness of the heat and humidity. He watched as Hardy and his deputies disappeared into the house, saw them pass by the open window, and then a few minutes later the three of them came out again. Hardy then came straight towards the *300* while the

81

other two stood talking on the porch. Bob saw them walking together back towards the SUV while he and Hardy backed out of the drive. Once out in the street, Hardy swung the car to go around to the other side of the hill.

"They've got to get photos of everything," Hardy said rather off-handedly, as if he thought Bob was curious, or maybe he himself just didn't want the silence. "Get samples from the floor, that kind of thing. Dr. Dave will process all the rest."

"What about the remains?" Bob asked.

"Dr. Dave will have to do an autopsy. But after that, we'll see to proper services. I'll make sure Father Jacob is fully involved."

By car, the Aloise home was about as far to the other side of the hill as you could go, a little more than two miles, and then another half-mile or so in off of Sylvan, down a narrow, winding road, trees dense all along the way. At the end of that lane was a small cul-de-sac around which there were three other houses, all of which went up at a much later date. The Aloise house was some distance before the cul-de-sac, set back to the right and off an elbow, leaving it somewhat isolated from those neighbors. It was something which suited Bob just fine. Close enough to say hello, far enough not to be a constant nuisance.

To the back of the Aloise house was where the hill was the steepest and the highest, rising almost one-hundred feet, and accessible pretty much only by a narrow trail, which though turning through the dense woods lazily left and right alternately, mainly to make the steepness more navigable, ran otherwise straight up.

As Hardy pulled the *300* up the dirt driveway, Bob pointed to the far side of the house. "Darla's over there," he said.

HUNGRY

Hardy followed Bob's finger, more out of reflex than anything else. Trying to sound as hopeful as possible, he said, "You know, it might not have been her."

Bob's tone was flat. "I can only hope." He was feeling guilty about the last thoughts he had about Darla and their marriage. He really did love her.

When Hardy had stopped the car, pulling up to the back of Bob's pickup, he suggested that Bob go check the house. "I'll take a walk around the side and have a look."

Bob hesitated only momentarily, the image of Dr. Lisa—or what was left to her—there on the lawn. "You come and tell me, okay?"

Hardy waited for Bob to make his way up the front porch and into the house. The door wasn't locked. As soon as he was in, Hardy strode across the front lawn, which hadn't been mowed too recently, and around the side of the house. The side yard was an expansive swath of relatively flat and grassy property—also left to grow, no less than two hundred feet long and at least a hundred wide. It ran off the front yard with a long, bending sweep following the flow of the road. At the far end, the tree line started again, running along the entire edge of the property and then up the hill as far as the eye could see. The entire back yard, too, was edged by trees, beyond which the hill climbed suddenly upwards. Hardy wondered if all of it belonged to Aloise. But then again, if it didn't, it probably would have been developed by now. Not that it mattered, but he thought he'd check with the deed office when he had the time.

It didn't take Hardy long to find the remains of Darla, although looking at what was there, he couldn't be sure it was her. Like the other victims, the head was gone, and there was nothing lying about that would suggest arms. Ribs he saw, and the spinal

HUNGRY

column, pelvis bones, and what looked to be the tibias and fibulas, one set of which was still attached to the femur. The other leg was in three sections, with each nearby to the others. He noted, too, that the collar bone had been scarred, and that all of the organs were gone. Not wanting to have Bob come identify his wife, he instead bent and picked up a few strips of tattered and shredded cloth. He tried to choose pieces not splattered or soaked with blood.

Hardy then made his way around the back of the house, had every intention of going in through the back door. That's when he noticed the grass was disturbed, sort of flattened here and there as if someone or something had been rolling in it. Crouching down, he found several patches of hair he thought to be dog, probably Ruff. However, none of them were impressive clumps, and there were no indications of blood or skin. The way he saw it, Ruff must have tangled with one of these things, held his own, at least for a while, and then got away while the getting was good. Maybe, he thought, that's why Bob was able to get away, too. The two he saw initially were too busy eating to bother, and the third one had its hands full with Ruff. He glanced about to see if the dog was anywhere in sight. Saw nothing. Standing back up, he said to himself, voice low but aloud, 'Now, if I could only figure out what was going on with the heads? Why were the heads missing? And why the arms?'

Entering the house through the back door, Hardy found Bob sitting at the kitchen table and drinking from a short glass.

Looking up as Hardy entered, Bob said, "I know it's early, but I really needed this. There's a glass there in the cabinet, if you want." He pointed to the left of the range hood.

HUNGRY

Hardy was tempted. "No, better not. I have to go over and talk to the Torres kid, at least take a statement, see how he's taking it."

Bob nodded, didn't say anything.

"Do me a favor, Bob. Don't go out there." He then remembered the pieces of cloth he had wadded up in his hand. He went over to the table, placed them down and smoothed them out gently. "I guess there's no good way to do this, Bob. Would you say Darla was wearing this?"

There was no doubt. "I hated that shirt," he said. "It was old and ratty. She said she liked it, it was really comfortable. I think she wore it just to get a rise out of me. It's not like we couldn't afford nice things."

It was Hardy's turn to nod. "Like I said, Bob. Don't go out there. I'll have someone over here right off. They'll do the official thing and then we'll get her taken to Dr. Dave. You know he'll treat her gentle, and then you'll be able to make arrangements. Let me know if there's anything I can do to help."

Bob finished off the glass. His face was grim and his lips tight. "Thanks, Harvey."

As Harvey started towards the front door, he said, "By the way, it looks like from what I found that Ruff got away. He probably took off up into the hills somewhere. I'm sure he'll come back as soon as he feel's safe. You might want to go call him; see if he'll come."

Bob's expression didn't change much, but Hardy did see a bit of a spark in his eyes.

"I have to make some other calls first," Bob said. Hardy knew he was referring to his kids.

The sheriff didn't spend long at the Torres house. The boy, Peter, didn't come across at all as if traumatized in any way. From the way he told it to Hardy, he first went up to the door to knock, to let Mr. Steed know he was there to mow the lawn. When no one answered, he first thought about going home, telling his mom there was no one there, and perhaps go back later. But then, he also knew that the shed was never locked and where Mr. Steed kept the fob to start the ride-on. Besides, Mr. Steed paid well for the job, and Peter wanted the money. It was when he was making his way around the side of the house that he noticed the blood on the grass, and then what he immediately recognized as a partial skeleton.

"There wasn't much left to it," he told Hardy. "And there wasn't all that much blood either. At first, I thought it might be the remains of a deer, something like that. Something the coyotes got. But when I saw the shirt all torn like that—at least it looked like it had been a shirt, well, I think I knew then it wasn't a deer. But I didn't think it was Mr. Steed, not then. And that's when I ran home."

Hardy wrote down the boy's statement, and then before leaving suggested that Alba keep the kids close to the house, reminded Peter it would not be a good idea for the time being to go anywhere near the Steed house, and to stay out of the hills. He also asked Alba that, if the chance arose, she let her neighbors know there might be something dangerous, some kind of animal, perhaps a few of them, coming down out of the hills. "Be careful, and keep an eye out." He then turned to Peter, and with a wink said, "If you see anything, be sure to give me a call."

After leaving the Torres house, he first went back to Barry's house, and then to Dr. White's house. He caught up with Dr. Dave there, and together they agreed that the doctor would need a couple of hours to examine the remains and see what he could come up with.

86

HUNGRY

"If I know anything sooner," the doctor said, "I'll call you directly."

"I'm very sorry," Hardy said. "I know you and Lisa White were very close, and how much you liked the boy."

Dave acknowledged the sheriff with a pat on the shoulder. "I'll call you."

HUNGRY

Dr. Dave

Dr. David Skylark learned to accept early in his professional career that being the doctor in a small town came with wearing multiple hats. Among them were that of coroner and, when required, forensic scientist assisting the local authorities. Rarely, however, had he ever been asked to wear both at the same time. The fact that the situation involved his co-worker and very close friend, Dr. Lisa White, made it all that much more difficult. Not to mention having to process emotionally the deaths of young Andy, Barry Steed and Darla Aloise, and in such a gruesome manner. It was all he could do to remain professional, and at the same time the only thing shielding him from what he was really feeling inside.

He had only been at the clinic for a handful of minutes, the coffee not yet brewed, when he received the first call from Tanya over at the police station. When she had told him Sheriff Hardy wanted him out at Barry Steed's place, well, he immediately realized before she said another word it had to be that Barry had died. His first thought was heart attack, but that would have required an ambulance. Were that the case, he would already have been aware. No ambulance went out without him knowing. And if it wasn't going to be local jurisdiction, the body would be on the way to the city hospital.

So, no, he wasn't really surprised when she said it was some kind of accident, perhaps an animal attack. He was aware that coyotes had become more brazen of late, and that sightings had increased. In fact, only a day or two ago, Katy Hastings' dog was attacked right there in her own backyard. Feisty old-bag that she was, she went out there with broom in hand and chased the coyotes off. Medicine woman or not, the truth is she was lucky there was only a pair of them, or they might have turned on her, too. But Barry Steed? Granted he was older. But still a pretty big guy, and he had that shotgun of his. There had to be something more to it.

And there was.

By the time Dr. Dave arrived at the Steed property, two of Hardy's deputies were already there, both vehicles, an SUV and a sedan, parked in the driveway one behind the other. It was Jeremy Strand that walked down to the road to greet him, while the other deputy, Kenny Dell, whose older brother Matt was also a deputy, was over in the side yard up by the garage. He had a collection of evidence bags but had yet to gather anything.

"We were waiting for you, Dr. Dave," said Jeremy, extending his hand. He was wearing rubber gloves. "It's over here." He pointed to where Deputy Dell was standing.

"By 'it' I presume you mean Barry Steed."

Jeremy nodded. "What's left of him."

"That's nice."

Jeremy caught the tone. "I don't mean any disrespect, Doc. It's just that...well, you can see for yourself."

Ultimately, Dr. Dave directed the use of a full body bag, but the volume of content hardly merited the space. He also had the two deputies gather any loose pieces of clothing material into an evidence bag, and take samples of the blood-covered grass. "Just to be sure," he said, meaning that the blood belonged to Barry Steed.

"Did you look around for the head?" He asked.

"Didn't find any sign of it. It looks, though, as if whatever got him went off that way and up into the hills." Jeremy was pointing to some trees along the edge of the property across from the

89

garage. "There's blood on the ground up that way. Can't say how far it goes; I only went in a short distance. Trees get thick not too far up, and the climb gets steep. I marked the area."

Dr. Dave could see a ribbon of yellow tape hanging motionless from a low branch.

"Any idea what may have done this, Doc?" Asked Kenny, securing the top of the bag holding some of the grass.

Dr. Dave shook his head. "No idea. From the looks of it, given the amount of lost body mass, there must have been more than one, and whatever it was has some sharp teeth and some awfully powerful hands, claws even. From my guess, poor Barry had both arms torn from the sockets, flesh and all. Popped the biceps tendons, complete rupture of both shoulder capsules, whole deal. A big bear could do something like that, but the teeth marks on the ribs, and on the leg bones, too, well, those aren't bear teeth. Could be some kind of canine. Wolves, maybe. But that still wouldn't explain the arms. And what would they do with the head? I could see a bear, or even a large mountain lion, cracking the skull open to get to the brain. But to decapitate the man, and then take off with the head. No, I don't see it. Maybe after I get a better look back at the clinic, I'll be able to tell you more. Anyway, you had better tape this area off. We don't need anybody wandering about."

No sooner had Dr. Dave got back into his car, the arrangements made to have Barry's remains transported back to the clinic, he received that second call from Tanya. Sheriff Hardy needed him over at Lisa White's house. Tanya told him it was bad, both Dr. Lisa and her son Andy. Looked like the same type of attack; and yes, both had been killed.

He had expected Hardy to be there when he arrived, but instead found his son David and young Eric Swan. Both were standing to the road side of their SUV and a good distance from the lawn and driveway.

"Glad you're here, doc," said David with the nod of his head. "I don't like seeing them like that, just sitting there on the driveway and in the grass."

Dr. Dave went over first to Andy's remains and then to Lisa's. With both heads gone, and given the amount of lost tissue, it was hard to be sure it was Andy and Lisa he was looking at, not that he doubted. The ribs and spinal column by the Cherokee were consistent with a boy Andy's age and build, and the shredded cloth scattered about the remains there in the grass were definitely Lisa's scrubs, or at least scrubs from the clinic.

Nevertheless, it was something he wasn't yet ready to accept. He had been working beside Dr. Lisa for more than fifteen years. They were more than just colleagues; they were as near to being family as could be without actually sharing blood. So pure and wholesome was their relationship that his own wife, Gayle, insisted that Lisa and the kids were part of their every holiday, to the extent that they routinely imposed themselves during Maggie's and Andy's birthdays, and were always welcomed. And if Dave was late getting home, and the reason was that he and Lisa had gone to dinner, or even out to have a drink at the *Bent Arrow*, Gayle never gave it a second thought. Nor should she have. To Dr. Dave, it was akin to a big brother/little sister relationship, even if he was closer in age to being her father, if not quite.

And now, not only were both Lisa and Andy dead, it was in a way that was particularly gruesome, utterly horrifying, and without regard for their person. Degrading, he thought it. He couldn't imagine what was going through their minds at the time, but was thankful in the knowledge that given the intensity of the attack, the state of shock would have been so complete that neither one of them probably felt too much in the way of pain.

"Where's Maggie?" He asked.

David answered. "Sheriff Hardy said something about her going to stay with a friend."

"I believe it was Carly Branch," added Eric.

Dr. Dave pressed his lips tight. "Good. I hope she didn't see any of this."

David looked down at his feet. "I think she did; some part of it, anyway. From what I understand, she was saved by Bob Aloise. Which reminds me, the sheriff asked me to send you over to the Aloise place. Apparently, whatever did this attacked Bob's wife Darla, also. It's pretty much like this over there, too."

Dr. Dave couldn't believe what he was hearing. "Another one?"

Jeremy nodded. "Seems there were four attacks in all."

As arranged, Sheriff Hardy rolled by Dr. Dave's office right around lunch time. A little later than noon, the sky remained overcast with low clouds, but there was that hint of brightness which suggested as much rain as was going to fall had already fallen. What drizzle there was had just about stopped and the breeze coming from the hill tops, lighter and cooler.

The front door of the clinic was open, the recessed lighting over the reception area bathing the waiting room in a pale amber glow, the air conditioning welcomed. At the desk sat Sandy, both nurse and receptionist, thumbing through some forms on a clipboard while glancing occasionally at the desk monitor.

"Hey, Sheriff Hardy," she said as he strode toward her. "Dr. Dave is expecting you. He said to send you back when you got here."

92

HUNGRY

Hardy returned Sandy's greeting with a tip of his hand. "Been busy today?" He asked.

Sandy shook her head. "Actually, kind of quiet. I guess with all the excitement…" She hesitated a moment, self-conscious as to her choice of words.

Hardy noticed. "It's okay. I know what you mean."

Sandy smiled sheepishly. "Well, anyway, I guess no one's giving too much thought to their own aches and pains."

Hardy nodded, his lips pressed thin. "He's in his office?"

"Back in the lab. You know the way?"

Again, Hardy nodded. "Short day?" He asked as he passed her by, heading towards the narrow hallway that led to the back of the building.

Sandy gave him that 'I wish' look. "Nah. I'm here to midnight. But Joshua will be here soon." She was grinning.

Joshua was the handsome, young intern, soon to be a full-fledged doctor himself.

"Good kid, that one," said Hardy. Joshua was born and bred.

Dr. Dave was finishing up a bite to eat when Hardy knocked on his door. He pushed the paper plate aside and touched up the sides of his mouth with a napkin. "Come on in. It's open." He tossed the plate and the remaining scraps into the tall garbage bin beside the lab table.

Hardy saw the organized clutter atop the table, the containers and clear dishes with their samples, the fancy and highly technical imaging cameras, the high definition monitors, the lap-top and desk-top, and everything else that reminded him of how old he was getting.

"You'd think there'd be an old-fashioned microscope among all this shit," he said.

HUNGRY

Dr. Dave laughed. "You're looking at one," he said, giving a quick point to the imaging camera. "A hundred times more effective, and I don't have to squint through a little eyehole."

Dave brought the monitor to life. It filled with an image that was every inch science.

"So, what am I looking at?" asked Hardy.

Dr. Dave prefaced by saying, "Keep in mind, I haven't had a whole bunch of time to go into this, so what I'm telling you is really superficial." He then went on. "What you're looking at on the monitor is a sample I took from Lisa's house. One of them. I took some from the stairs going up to the second floor, from the wood floor in the living room, from a shard of glass from the picture window, and from out on the front porch." He clicked through all four.

To Hardy they all looked the same. "And?"

Dr. Dave shrugged. Picking up a pen, he pointed to specific areas of the image. "You see this here?" He asked. He didn't wait for a response. "Were I to make an educated guess, I'd say these are red blood cells. Only they're not red, and I'm not even one hundred percent sure it's blood." He went on before Hardy could interrupt. Moving his pen, he said, "And these here, I'd say these are white blood cells. But again, I'm only going on assumptions based on logic. You see, in us, for example, or most mammals, the red blood cells are much larger than these. And they look somewhat different. We, meaning humans and mammals in general, tend to have more white blood cells by volume than I'm finding here. That said, I'm willing to go out on a limb and say this *is* a sample of blood, or at least a blood-like plasma. But not like any I've ever seen."

Hardy took advantage of Dr. Dave's pause to get a word in edge-wise. "Anything you've ever seen in mammals?"

94

"Anything I've ever seen anywhere."

"So, what are you saying? We're not dealing with an animal? At least, not one that we know of?"

Dave shrugged. "Give me a chance to do some thinking aloud here, and then tell me what you think. Everything organic is defined by its environment. Beast, bird, fish, insects, whatever, they're evolved to survive in their particular surroundings. Only man has managed to overcome his physical limitations to impose himself wherever he wishes, more or less. From these samples, it is obvious that we're looking at something both organic and on a lower developmental scale when compared to us. So no, animal is a good start. That said, these red blood cells—and again, they are not red—are either highly efficient or highly inefficient. As you know, red blood cells carry oxygen throughout our system. Well, these are way too small to do the job efficiently; that is if they were in us. But, say they were to be in an oxygen-poor environment in which little oxygen was available, or even required. It may be that they are designed to transport and use the oxygen they carry more efficiently, or that the body in which they function has different requirements when it comes to that oxygen. I can't tell from the samples. As expected, they're oxygen depleted. And without a body, I can't make any guesses about its needs. What I will suggest is that in terms of origin, we're talking a very thin atmosphere; not to the extent of a vacuum, but much closer to that than this." He flipped his hand to take in their surroundings.

Hardy let out a sigh. "It's not that I don't follow you, Dave. I get all that. What I don't get is what you're getting at. It sounds as if you're talking about something ET."

Dave's expression didn't change. "I don't know about extraterrestrial, but definitely alien."

Hardy knew Dave was an open-minded guy, and generally serious, especially when it came to his profession. "I assume, of course, that you looked at the bite marks? The wounds and damage to the bones?"

"Of course."

"And you're positive it's nothing from around here?"

Dave shook his head. "I mean teeth are teeth," he started. "And whatever did this is a predator. These attacks were not defensive or in response to provocation. These animals were hunting. The severe loss of tissue combined with no evidence of any tissue in the nearby vicinity suggests feeding. But if you're thinking this was bear, or wolf, or coyotes, or even a mountain lion—no way. I compared the bite marks and gash to bone to everything that I had on hand." He tapped the side of the monitor. "With this thing here, I can immediately access any animal known to man, and with a couple of clicks be looking at side by side comparisons. We're talking about clear differences in length, depth, spacing, angle of penetration…you name it. Nothing matches."

"Doesn't leave me all that much to go on."

"At least you don't have to worry about a serial killer or a mass murderer."

Hardy smiled; there was no humor in it. "There is that."

Dr. Dave made a vague gesture towards the items arranged on the table. "All I can tell you, Harvey, is that I'll continue to look." His face then took on a more sullen expression. "In meantime, what do you want me to do with the remains? I'm sure the families will want to get on with the services."

"You have everything you need right?" Harvey was referring to samples and photos.

Dr. Dave nodded.

"No problem," Harvey said, his face grim and his lips pressed tight. He turned to leave. "Send me over the reports as soon as you can, okay Doc?"

"Soon as I can."

As he went out the door and into the hallway, Harvey heard Dr. Dave say something about Gayle and helping out Maggie, but his mind was elsewhere, thinking it would be useful to make a call to his son at the university. While he might have some ideas as an anthropologist, Harvey was thinking it was his significant other, his partner, lover, however it was they referred to their arrangement, that might be the bigger help. If he recalled correctly, his son said she was a Zoologist, or something of the sort. Harvey tapped his chest for his phone, came up flat. He had the image of it sitting on the front seat of the *300*.

HUNGRY

Father Jacob

It was the death of the boy, Andy, which got to Father Jacob more so than the others. He could rationalize those, if not so much Dr. Lisa as Darla Aloise and Barry Steed. They, the three of them, were adults, at least. To some degree, they had their chance. They got to experience adulthood and how shitty and unfair life could be…was.

And Father Jacob was not a pessimist. He wasn't a hater of life. To the contrary. He loved being alive, more so because he knew in his heart, his soul—to him little more than an expression—that this was all there was of Paradise or, for that matter, Hell. Funny thing for a priest to think; more than think but believe, and more yet, to believe as a rational truth.

He had received a call late in the afternoon. It came from Tanya down at the Sheriff's office. She gave him only some of the details. But it was enough. He said he'd be there straight off. She told him to go to the clinic, that the remains were there. She told him, too, that it would be disturbing, and that he should not expect to see the deceased.

Still, he wasn't prepared. It's just not possible to give last rights to a body bag and feel that you were meeting the expectations of the deceased.

He said as much to Dr. Dave. Dave told him it wouldn't make any difference, really. "I'm afraid, Father, none of them have their heads."

It was all Father Jacob could do to stifle the laugh he felt vibrating down deep in his diaphragm, and it wasn't because he thought any of this was funny. It was an emotional reflex. He was prone to such things.

HUNGRY

Father Jacob wasn't always a Soldier of God. He had far greater aspirations in his youth than he managed to maintain now that he was fifty. A Jesuit, he studied in Guatemala, after which he spent a number of years ministering to the poor and needy in that country. It bothered him to say it aloud, so he rarely did, but the whole thing kind of wore thin.

He himself had not been brought up in poverty, but instead in a more traditional middle-class Catholic family in Canada, Ontario actually. His father had a municipal job and his mother was an elementary school teacher. Jacob played sports: baseball, hockey, basketball, was popular in high school, lost his virginity in tenth grade, and had every intention of doing something extraordinary with his life. He even applied and accepted to, and then attended a semester in Binghamton. His first impression of New York State.

And then something happened for which he had no clear explanation. He found religion could be something beyond that of his upbringing, which was superficial at the best: catechism, confirmation, church on Christmas and Easter, lent and ashes, and not using the Lord's name in vain.

Even to this day, he's not really sure what happened. It was following a particularly heavy weekend of on-campus/off-campus partying, one in which he was drinking and toking and falling into bed with any girl who was both ready and willing. It was all about the physical pleasure, the heat of the moment. Amazing, he thought, even in the process of thrusting his hips, that there was nothing intimate about the act. He could honestly say that there was never a connection between him and his sexual partner. For all it mattered to him, they could have been a couple of hamsters. How often he thanked God for not knocking one of them up, given the selfishness of it all, and saddling some kid with a life he or she would never understand.

HUNGRY

The next thing he knew, he had made his mind up that the extraordinary thing he was to do was give his life over to God. And so, he discovered the Jesuits. Less than a month later he had talked his parents into the whole Guatemala trip, and not being able to speak any more than third-year high school Spanish, he enrolled in Jesuit school and was living thousands of miles from home.

At first, he thought it was just a matter of homesickness, of wanting to sleep in a real bed, take a real shower, see real buildings, buy food in a supermarket, or even watch a Major League baseball game or the NBA. Whatever it was, without much fanfare, and without telling anyone he was leaving or coming, he was on a plane and it was landing in big city, Canada.

He moved back in with his parents for a short spell, but ultimately took a position in a Canadian school run by the Jesuits on a Native Indian reservation, and for a while was generally happy. But a grown man can't be living in a school rectory with a handful of other grown men, not to mention making a salary which only made ends meet because they weren't that far apart in the first place.

While contemplating his next move, one of the other Jesuits with whom he was teaching happened to mention having received the opportunity to go the States, to New York, not too far south of the border, to take over the ministry of a small parish upon a reservation. It was Mohawk and in what was called the *Valley*. Very unique opportunity, it seemed. But the Jesuit to whom it was offered wasn't overly interested, having settled quite nicely into the routine he currently had. One thing led to another, and less than a month later, Father Jacob, who had some familiarity with the Mohawks, was in the Valley.

That was twenty-three years ago.

HUNGRY

He learned upon his arrival that the valley had been settled during the revolutionary war, and since that time it had been a Jesuit to serve the community as priest and leader of the religious flock, as it were. He was both welcomed and at the same time provided his own space. A significant member of the community, he was nonetheless apart from it, in as much as everyone else was Native American and he was not. It was a role and distinction he enjoyed, as his title shined a particular light upon him, while allowing him to otherwise move within shadows. He was treated well, respected, included in all social aspects of community life, yet at the same time, left alone and allowed his privacy. He was a Soldier of God, and that was all the people of the community expected of him.

Up until the last few years, Father Jacob felt renewed and vital. He enjoyed his relationship with God. He kept up with the *Word*. He truly believed that he was accountable for souls, and more so, for helping his parishioners frame their own personal understanding of the inevitable. To him, it didn't matter what impression a person had of Heaven, of the after-life, only that they were comfortable with that impression.

He even made the effort to skirt any reference to a celestial paradise, to a New Jerusalem, to the second-coming, or anything related to *Revelation*—Christianity's most obvious work of propaganda. His emphasis remained the here-and-now, physical contact with the physical world. He felt he was doing no disservice to the *Word* by working to bring people peace of mind, to minimize the ever-present whisper of the inevitable. It was his own *dulcificación de la muerte*.

And then came Sandy Hook. And then not much later, the Tsarnaev brothers and the Boston Marathon bombings. It wasn't the events themselves which dissolved the veneer of his

101

conviction. When confronted with these types of senseless happenings, Father Jacob had long since stopped asking God, Why? He simply accepted they were random, as random as life itself. He even stopped the virtual rolling of his eyes, the virtual smirks, whenever people accepted them with a shrug and one of those distancing statements, such as, 'God works in mysterious ways' or 'God has a plan for all of us'. He'd adopt the expected facial expression and nod his head, but to himself think, 'horseshit'.

No, what got to him was a certain bit of surreal absurdity in each case which reduced to smoke and mirrors, at least for him, all that was manifested by the *Word*.

The first was the vigil the mourning community held in a church literally across the way from the Sandy Hook school. Why? So that they could take comfort in God's proximity, of course. That's what they said: God's proximity. God's presence, physically, spiritually, was right there in that church, accessible to their pain and confusion. How then to explain His overtly conspicuous absence but a few strides away, there in the hallways of that elementary school, while Adam Lanza was shooting rounds of ammunition into the little bodies of first and second-graders? Surely, there is no mystery or plan so encompassing that its fulfillment in anyway is dependent upon the slaughter of twenty innocent and naïve six and seven year-olds: so terrified, so confused, and so brutally dispatched.

The second was the words of a middle-aged gentleman, a response he had for a TV reporter. Standing literally across the street from where the first Tsarnaev pressure-cooker exploded, he said, with a practiced tone of conviction and faith, 'I am so thankful that God was watching over my family.' His family, according to what he said, had been seated in the temporary stands located on that spot and no more than thirty feet or so from an eight-year old boy being torn to pieces by burning shrapnel. How convinced this grown man was that God's hand had been extended that moment over the heads of his loved ones, but not acknowledge that in the process, that same omnipresent, omnipotent and all-knowing God elected to keep his back turned to the violent decomposition of an innocent eight-year-old. That's what bothered Father Jacob.

After that, Father Jacob let himself become a caricature of the profession, a cliché. It was a transition which required no specific effort on his part. He simply became what it was his parish expected him to be. He was the *Word of God* personified. He was a service provider and he was financially compensated. He had the church. He had the small cottage that came with it. He had ample property to roam. And his life was compartmentalized. He was the priest when he was required to be the priest. He was Jacob otherwise. And the people of the valley saw him only in the light, and paid no attention when he moved among the shadows.

After he left the clinic, Father Jacob went first to see Maggie. He thought it best to do so when his energy levels were high, fully expecting her to be the more emotional. He had known Bob Aloise to be somewhat stoic and macho, though a man strong in his faith and conviction, and presumed he'd show the same degree of resiliency once he made his way over to the house. Better to go downhill, he said to himself.

He met Maggie at the Branch household. She was staying there for the time being, but Dr. Dave has said something about her perhaps moving in with them. Nothing had been decided yet; it was more just a conversation between him and Gayle. "I'm not sure how she feels about it," Dr. Dave had said.

HUNGRY

Monica and Carly Branch were there when Father Jacob arrived. It was Monica who met him at the door, greeting him with sad, doe eyes and an expression to match.

"Come on in, Father," she said. "Maggie is out on the back deck with Carly. She's doing as best as can be expected, poor dear."

Father Jacob followed in her wake, down the open hallway leading past the living room on one side and an ample family room on the other, all with natural wood floor to ceiling, and into the kitchen. There were sliding glass doors straight ahead, and plenty of yellow sunlight spilling across the floor. They exchanged small talk along the way, neither one of them addressing the killings.

As soon as Father Jacob stepped out on to the deck, Carly stood from her chair, gave Maggie a smile, and said she'd be inside if Maggie needed her. She then greeted Father Jacob with relative cheer, patted his hand as she went by, and she and Monica went back inside.

"We're right inside, Maggie," she said, being supportive.

It sounded to Father Jacob as if they were anticipating the Inquisition.

Maggie, contrary to what he had anticipated himself, was quite contained. Her eyes were red from crying, and her face somewhat puffy, but other than that there were no demonstrations of emotional breakdown or uncontrolled sobbing.

"I saw them, Father," she said, her eyes to the hands folded in her lap and then her head turning slowly to look up at him. "Mom was on the front lawn. Those things were eating her. Andy was in the driveway, right next to the car. He was face down. His clothes had been ripped away, but there didn't seem to be anything left to him. I saw his bones, his spine, I think. I can still see it all in my head, but as if a dream, as if I know what I'm looking at, but I'm

104

not really seeing it." Her words came slow and measured, distant, but strong and clear.

"It must have been horrible for you, Maggie. I'm so sorry." Father Jacob knew that acknowledgement was most effective for encouraging Maggie to keep talking.

"I wanted to do something, Father. To make them stop. I tried to. But Mr. Aloise pulled me away. After that we ran, after they tried to get us, too."

Maggie's words were suddenly beseeching, halting and shaped from loss.

Father Jacob wanted to tell her there was nothing she could have done. Nothing would have changed the outcome. From what he was told by Dr. Dave, both Lisa and Andy most likely died very quickly. Regardless, they were definitely dead by the time Maggie came upon them.

Instead he said, "Your mom and your brother are beyond any pain and suffering now, Maggie. I'm so very sorry that you saw what you saw. And I wish I could take it away from you. And I promise, as painful and as confusing as it is now, I will help you through it."

"I don't think that's possible," she said, a tear sliding down her cheek.

He thought of appropriate scripture, said only, "I know, Maggie. I know."

They sat silently for a while later, an appreciated breeze sweeping down the hill and across the deck, the leaves up in the trees whispering secret words neither could catch.

"Were they demons?" Asked Maggie, her eyes searching his.

"Demons?" He repeated. "No, Maggie, I don't think so. I'm not sure demons exist, not in that way. Not Hell sent or evil."

HUNGRY

Maggie wasn't convinced. "I saw them father. They came for me. And one of them came through the picture window and into the house. Mr. Aloise shot at it. They weren't like anything I've ever seen before. Not any animal. It was like a science-fiction movie, or a *Stephen King* horror novel, only real."

"I wish I had an answer for you, Maggie. And I'm sure Sheriff Hardy will do everything he can to find whatever did this." He wished he had a better answer.

They spoke a little longer. By the time Father Jacob felt it was proper to leave, he was satisfied that he was of some comfort, and more still that Maggie had the inner-strength to get through this. He left feeling it would definitely be best that she went to live with Dr. Dave and Gayle, better so than remaining with the Branches. The Branches were a nice family. But Maggie didn't need nice. She needed support and comforting, and she needed these things long term. She'd get it from Dave and Gayle. He'd make it a point to have that conversation with the two of them, and soon. He left Maggie with his cell number and promised he'd be back to see her the next day.

No sooner did he make his way back into the kitchen, Carly slipped out to be with Maggie.

Monica asked Father Jacob how it went. He gave her the answer he knew she wanted.

"I'm glad, Father," she said as she walked him out front.

Bob Aloise was much simpler. He thanked Father Jacob for coming, offered him a beer. Father Jacob accepted. There was some reminiscing as they sat at the kitchen table, that same breeze blowing through the open windows. Aloise told him he had spoken with his children, and of course they were all coming home for the service. He spoke to Father Jacob about being with Maggie, about being there just in the nick of time, of saving her and pulling her into the house, and about their taking shelter for the night in the shed. It broke his heart, he said, knowing that Maggie had to have seen what had happened to her mother and little brother, and how angry it made him.

"I know I shot one of those devils," he said, a somewhat manic grin twisting his normally easy-going features. "There was blood all over the place. If you can wound them, you can kill them. Hardy mentioned something about going out to have a look. If he'll have me, I'm going to go along. Got my hunting rifle loaded and ready to go." Bob gestured with a hooked thumb over his shoulder.

Father Jacob didn't see any gun. "I think I'll come along, too," he said.

Bob nodded. "Can't hurt any to have a priest along when you're hunting devils."

The *Word*. Father Jacob nodded.

They finished their beers in short order, and then Father Jacob took his leave.

"Keep the service short, heh, Father?" Bob smiled.

Father Jacob took it as it was meant. "You just wink if I go on too long," he said.

Bob winked.

HUNGRY

The Barrow

The alpha looked up from the kill upon which it was feeding, saw new prey well within reach. But his hunger close to sated, he lacked the instinct to pounce. The other two males, however, were younger and eager to the chase. They turned from Dr. Lisa's remains, came up out of the crouch and leaped forward.

The alpha, there in the driveway, saw sudden movement from the cave-not-a-cave. It was another of their kind. Bigger and more physical than the prey already taken, it descended out onto the lawn and scooped up the other, the smaller one. A moment later, they were both gone, retreating into the cave-not-a-cave and only their scent lingering behind.

He watched, then, as the lesser of the two younger males moved in pursuit, the other more cautious. The lesser male flared his nostrils wide, snuffing up the scent from the ground. Then with one effortless leap was up the porch steps, his snout pushed forward and his hands pawing at the air. Up against the front door of the house he went, pressing his mouth to it, intent on the prey.

Testing, he pawed at the surface, his nails sinking into the wood and gouging shallow furrows. Sidling to the left, he continued to sniffle and snuffle. Something caught his eye, a sudden ripple and a stab of light. The alpha saw it too. The lesser male pushed his snout across to the surface of the picture window, bared his teeth. Suddenly, there was a snap, sharp but not too loud. Then the glass skittering and bouncing as the pane gave way. The alpha's head filled with an image of sky fire sizzling and crackling across stone. But his eyes saw nothing of the sort. Then came two quick barks, stark and angry. The lesser male jumped back, and then jumped again. He hissed as if startled; he yipped as if with pain. And then he, too, was gone, leaping into the stabbing light, interrupted and distracting.

The second male made a move to follow. Looking back at the alpha, he hesitated. Understanding and obeying, he held his ground, eased back to a less tense crouch.

The alpha lifted its nose and whiffed at the air. He caught the familiar musk of the two remaining males of the clan, knew them to be near. The second male caught it, too. He turned and went back to his kill. Without a second glance at the cave-not-a-cave or a concern for the whereabouts of the lesser male, he gathered up Lisa's two arms in one hand and her head in the other. They were food for the females and the young one. The alpha did the same, retrieving the one arm of Andy's which it hadn't eaten, then his head, too.

Neither the alpha nor the second male looked back. The lesser male would join them or he wouldn't. Instead, they moved together across the driveway, past the small pile of Andy's discarded bones and sinew, the surprisingly little blood on the driveway, around the back end of the vehicle—the door still open wide, the bags of groceries undisturbed, and onto the lawn to the other side. As they did, the other two males materialized out of the darkness at the side of the house. Each carried some part of the remains of Darla Aloise and Barry Steed, including the head of each.

Together they crossed the side yard and made for the trees.

The young male was driven by the scent filling his nostrils. Ignoring the fire which burned in his stomach—and not because he was full, the twitching at the side of his head, the right eye through which he could no longer see, he moved forward. He crossed the wood floor of the living room and entered the kitchen.

HUNGRY

He recognized nothing, the bright glare causing him to look through his own fingers, to squint and blink.

He detected the faint scent of the creature he had taken down and eaten. He moved toward it. But then he caught the scent of the other one, the one the alpha had tackled and killed. So, he changed direction. Up he went, his breathing labored and his head starting to spin.

He followed the scent only so far. It was becoming stale and fading. Besides, the fire in his gut burned to the point of distraction, the weakness in his limbs stealing from his will. He stumbled once on the way back down. Retraced his own tracks, smelled himself in the air, his wounds. He smelled, too, more prey. But he didn't have it in him to follow. The musk of the alpha had dissipated with distance, and that of the other males, too. Now alone, he abandoned the hunt.

He made his way back out onto the porch, scrambling less than gracefully over the top of the couch and through the space where the picture window used to be. A shard of glass sticking up from the bottom of the sash sliced into his calf. He was aware but paid it no heed. Down the porch and onto the lawn, he stopped momentarily at Lisa's body, and then again where Andy lay. He was looking for something that wasn't there. He pawed at some of what remained, but moved on empty-handed.

He found the place between the trees where the alpha led, and he followed. But a few strides up the steep incline his lungs began to burn, his breaths short and halting. He pushed on, the musk of the clan lingering but fading. The ground underfoot was not what he was accustomed to. In an effort to maintain his balance, to keep his feet beneath him, he gulped at the air. It wasn't enough to keep him moving. He managed only a couple of strides at a time before he was forced to pause and rest. The scent of the others was lost, not due to distance but because his faculties were beginning to fail. It was he that couldn't find their scent, confused as it was among the many strange odors of this strange place. To make matters worse, there was a distracting sound building in his head, as if he was cuddled up deep within a tight space in the rock. The thought of sleep came to him.

Without thinking about it, he moved from the path he was on, often stumbling down upon one knee, and then reduced to dragging himself along the best he could. He found a place to conceal himself. Not that he knew to name it so, but it was a fallen tree, its thick trunk and the dirt impacted roots pulled up tall, overgrown with brush and tangled. Using his arms, he pulled himself across the ground and rolled himself out of sight. Breathing hard against the thickness of the air, he let his body go slack, felt his weight nestle deep into a blanket of dried leaves covering the warm ground. With no image filling his head, with only the tranquility of darkness closing in around him, he let his one eye close, having already forgotten he once had the use of the other.

Sleep came. The death.

The alpha stopped. The scent of the lair hung in the air. He held his position near a dense gathering of sugar maple, his eyes moving back and forth, waiting while the other three males went ahead, disappearing through a copse of thick brush and brambles.

The lair was beyond the old burial grounds, where back when the Earth was young a great slab of stone had fallen away and then was covered over again. The chaos had left behind a long narrow barrow which burrowed back into the hills and down into the darkness. If any had ever found it, it was long ago and beyond the memory of those living in the valley.

111

HUNGRY

For the alpha, though, it may as well have been put there for this very purpose. No sooner had he set out to find shelter, that terrible glare growing more intense by the moment, he heard the song of its echo like an incessant beat with a single measure.

Normally, he would have gone off on his own, the clan waiting behind in some concealed hallow or to the back of tall stone. But the growing glare made him uneasy in a way he had never felt. They knew to follow.

There were things all around them for which the alpha had no reference, no image buried somewhere deep within his memory to compare. His senses heightened, his nostrils were assaulted with alien scents, his ears with a continuous whisper—broken only by occasional whistles and barks, the flow of air into his lungs heavy and thick, a taste painting his tongue.

His hands held before his eyes to shade the ever-intensifying glare, the nagging ache pushing at his skull, the loss of form and depth, he did all he could to shut out all but the billowing from out of the empty space that pulled him forward. Barely aware of the presence of the clan members, he swam through the branches and brambles for which he had no name, the tangle of thorns snagging the resilient hair covering his limbs and torso, biting at the flesh beneath. And then the glare was gone, an enveloping darkness muting the outside world and easing the pain behind his brow.

It was there they waited out the glare in the sky. It was there they left the females and the young one to go out and hunt.

He felt safe there, comforted by its proximity to prey.

Sensing no danger, or the presence of prey or predator, the alpha gave one last sniff to the air. Within a few silent strides, he too was past the thin branches and tangles. The entrance to the barrow was close to the ground and to the shaded side of tall rock, most of which was layered with moss and draped with coiling vine with red edges—a color neither he nor his kind could distinguish.

Inside the barrow, mostly packed earth and lines of stone, and obligating him to stoop low as not to hit his head, he immediately located the females, their musk distinct from his own and from the males, including the young one. He smelled, too, the impending birth. It stirred his loins and drove him deeper into the lair.

Down he went, the way slopping ever so gently. To his right, the tunnel widened as if the soil had been scooped away, baring the stone to the floor and to the far wall. The expecting female was there, prone on her back, her knees up and apart. The other female sat beside her, sensing the immediacy of the birth. There, too, but an arm's length from them both were the four heads. As soon as the new-born came, the females would smash the skulls against the rock to get at the soft brain matter inside. The new-born would be hungry and require immediate nourishment. The arms were there, also. The females, too, needed to eat. Not only would the birthing be exhausting, but so, too, was the intense and feral coupling that would follow. And the alpha was ready.

Further down the tunnel, the other three clan males had enticed the young one with another of the limbs, whether Lisa's or Darla's or Andy's, it didn't matter. He took it gladly, scurried off to spot he claimed as his own, and was pulling off chunks of muscle and sinew with his hands and teeth.

The other males knew the smell of birth, also. And they, too, felt the stir in their loins. But it was not theirs to respond. At least, not until the alpha had his way. Then they, too—even the young one, would each approach the females to take their turn. In this way, the continuing of the clan was assured, and in this way, all newborns belonged to all of the clan.

113

HUNGRY

The baby was born with no more noise than the sound of its first breath. Passing between the female's legs, it lay motionless lest it attract the attention of a predator; not that it knew to do so. It just did, and would remain that way until the female took it up. Then it would open its mouth and wait to be fed.

The older female was already smashing the back of Andy's head against the rock, not violently but effectively, the remaining blood staining the stone, and the hair and the flesh folding away from the bone. With but a little more effort, the female was picking away tiles of white skull, and with long, agile fingers began extracting chunks of the brain. She handed them over to the birth mother, who gently placed pinch after pinch into the new one's eager mouth.

Sated, the new one was placed aside to sleep while the two females eagerly fed on the waiting limbs. No sooner had they consumed the fleshier parts and took to gnawing at the bone, the ligaments, the tendons, the alpha made his presence known. The new mother lay down on her side beside the new born, her back to the alpha. She pulled her knees up towards her chest and offered herself, curling her backside to the alpha. He lay down at her back and positioned his midsection, his maleness rigid and thrusting. He found her with practiced ease, entering her and penetrating as deeply as he could. It was not love-making; it was coupling: intense, aggressive and short in duration.

Finished, the alpha pulled out and away from the first female and turned towards the second. She had already assumed an accessible position, and he wasted no time. He climbed upon her, thrust his member into her, and if it took him any longer, it was only because the intensity was never the same the second or third time as it was the first. It had nothing to do with preference.

114

HUNGRY

His responsibility met, he left the two females to await the other males of the clan, and by himself went off into a dark stretch of the tunnel to sleep. He'd need his rest for the next hunt.

HUNGRY

Big Red Harrison

No sooner had they let the dog go, it took off at a run in the direction the alpha had led the other males, there where the deer trail climbed back into the hills.

"Go get'em, girl. That's my Sheba," extorted Big Red Harrison, his voice deep and hoarse. He then turned to Dave Hardy and Eric Swan. "Didn't I tell you she was good?"

Eric Swan had a stupid grin on his face, at least that's the way Dave interpreted it. "Yeah, leading us to a couple of wild turkeys or a rabbit," he laughed.

Eric glanced over to see Big Red's reaction. You didn't mess with Big Red. At least he wasn't going to. To him, the man was part legend, part bigger-than-life. Everyone in the valley knew Big Red. He had always been *the Man*, and every kid growing up in the valley knew you didn't mess with *the Man*. When he was on duty, you drove the speed limit, you didn't smoke out on the streets; hell, you wouldn't even jay walk if Big Red was watching.

But Big Red had no reaction whatsoever. He merely said, his tone above it all, "Well, we'll see. But you better make sure the safeties are off those rifles, boys."

Big Red had only the colt holstered at his hip. "I'm off-duty," is what he had said.

They set off at a leisurely pace to the edge of the trees, the dog's eager yips not all that far away, bouncing from one side then the other of the trail leading up.

"No need to hurry," said Big Red. "She'll let us know if she has something."

HUNGRY

Sheriff Hardy had reached out to Big Red earlier asking him to join them for the department debriefing, leaving a message when there was no answer. He had no doubt he'd show. Although officially retired, he was always around: once a deputy in the valley, always a deputy in the valley. And besides, he was the man with the dogs. Damn good animals those two when it came to hunting deer, or wild turkey, rabbits, raccoons, and even scaring off coyotes and the occasional overly curious bear. They might only be Labradors, friendly as hell, but they could raise up a racket when they wanted to, or bare teeth when necessary—and as convincing as any Shepherd or Doberman.

Big Red had showed up in his over-sized Dodge Ram, a toy he gave himself as a retirement gift, stepping out in full gear: hiking boots, a faded pair of Levi's, a long-sleeve shirt to keep the ticks off, and a brimmed hat matching the one he wore while a deputy—only without the flare. Almost a year to the day since he signed his papers, he hardly looked any different. His mid-section was still flat. His shoulders remained rounded in the right places and his back broad. His legs looked as sturdy as ever, and the long-sleeves did nothing to hide the thickness to his forearms. His dark hair remained short but bushy, if but with a hint of silvery-gray around the temples. Sheriff Hardy could only hope he looked so good when he turned seventy.

Hardy had just pulled into the lot coming back from Dr. Dave when he caught the milk white Ram in his side view mirror. He parked in the spot marked Sheriff, got out of the front seat, closed the door and stood just beside while Big Red walked over to him.

The two shook hands, and as they walked into the building, Hardy thanked him for coming and filled him in on the situation.

The five other deputies were already assembled in the conference room when Hardy and Big Red entered.

HUNGRY

By the end of the debriefing, they agreed they would separate into three parties. Jeremy and Kenny would work together and take one of the dogs. Big Red had said they could have Spartacus. "He's the more independent of the two," he said. They'd start over by Barry Steed's place and work up that side of the Hill. Dave and Eric Swan would go with Big Red and take the other dog on over to the White's place and work up the front of the Hill. Sheriff Hardy and Matt Dell would start at the Aloise place and work their way up the back of the Hill.

"We really have no idea what we're looking for," Hardy admitted. "But I have a feeling that if we find it, we'll know. The only witnesses we have are Bob Aloise and Maggie White. But what they saw, they saw in the dark. All I got out of it was that we're looking for something that moves on two legs, kind of looks like a somewhat smaller version of us, may or may not be covered in hair or fur, or something along those lines, and has yellowish-colored eyes with large, black pupils. If I can go by what Bob said, these things are definitely some kind of wild animal. Both he and Maggie mentioned, too, something about a smell. Musky, they said, maybe like something dead. So, keep your nose to the wind."

"Any idea how many of these things we're looking for?" Asked Jeremy, not yet sounding completely convinced it was anything other than coyotes, a cougar at the worse.

Hardy put his hands up. "No. From what Bob and Maggie said, I'm thinking at least three. But we've got four victims in three different places. Dr. Dave hasn't had the time to do anything more than preliminary stuff. So, I have no confirmation. But to me, if there were three of these things outside of the White's house, I have to believe there are others."

Dave raised up a hand, started his question at the same time. "Do we shoot?"

HUNGRY

Hardy sucked back on his teeth. "Yeah. We've got four dead already. Shoot to kill."

Dave and Eric reached the tree line first, paused where the deer trail started up, and waited for Big Red to catch up. Despite the rain that had fallen for most of the morning, there were still some traces of blood on the small leaves of the underbrush beside the tree. It was dark red, and from what the Sheriff had said about the samples Dr. Dave had looked at, probably belonging to Dr. Lisa or Andy, and not from the thing that Bob Aloise claimed to have shot.

Dave shook his head. There was a sadness in him. "Motherfuckers," he hissed beneath his breath but loud enough for the other two to hear.

"We'll get'em," said Big Red, a mix of compassion and conviction to his tone.

Just then, Sheba's barking came back to them, and this time more intense and excited than before.

Big Red chuckled. "Didn't I tell you? Hear that? She's onto something."

Dave and Eric looked over to him.

"Well, don't just stand there, boys. Get after it," he barked, every bit *the Man*.

They both responded without hesitation, leaning out ahead of long strides up the trail, steep like stairs but without the steps.

"I'm an old man," Big Red called to their backs. "I'll be right behind you." And then he started up at his own pace, grabbing at the nearest tree or branch as he went up and Sheba's excitement coming back to him from a distance, but from the sound of it, not all that far. "She's up there to a piece, boys. Somewhere there to the left."

119

HUNGRY

Dave was the first one to catch sight of the black Lab. Eric, though, could have overtaken him at any time. He was the quicker and more agile of the two. But Dave had the experience and was higher in the pecking order, so that's the way it was done. Let Dave get there first, and be right there at his back and ready for anything.

Sheba had gone off the deer trail and into the thicket some two-hundred yards up and well short of the top of the hill. From where Dave stood, Eric a short stride behind, he saw there was a tree that had gone down, a good-size sugar maple, more than an arm's reach around. When it had fallen, it had pulled up its roots and all the surrounding soil. By the looks of it, it had been there for a while. He could see a chaotic tangle of vines, dense with small spearhead leaves, dark green and tinged with red, and brush and brambles sticking up wherever space could be had.

Sheba was pawing at the ground, though he couldn't see all of her through the brush and thicket. She was whining, too, pushing her head forward and then bouncing back as if in momentary retreat, or unsure of what she had found.

Dave put up his hand to stop Eric, and together they stood and listened, both trying to get a better look through the leaves and branches.

After a second or two, Eric said, "I don't hear anything."

Dave nodded. "Only the damn dog."

"What do you think?"

Dave edged a step closer. "I'm going to go check it out. You stay behind me and be ready to shoot anything that moves that isn't me or the dog."

Eric wasn't as sure. "There's not much of an angle here." Meaning if he had to shoot.

"Well, get closer." Then he headed towards the fallen tree.

120

HuNGRY

Eric brought up the barrel of the rifle, made sure the safety was off. He let Dave get a number of strides ahead, and then he came up at his back, but at an angle to have a clear shot, if necessary.

Dave moved cautiously, picking his way the best he could through the underbrush, too much of which was laced with small but aggressive thorns. As he neared the spot, Sheba came eagerly to his side and nudged his thigh with her nose. She then turned and went back towards the fallen tree. From the angle he had, Dave could see that there was a hollow formed by the height of the root and trunk. He saw that there was something curled up within it, too. Whatever it was, it had some size and shape to it. There was no movement. He assumed, given the commotion Sheba was making, that it wasn't sleeping either.

"There's definitely something here," he called out to Eric, his voice a loud whisper.

"What do you think it is?"

"It ain't no wild turkey, I'll tell you that much."

Eric didn't want Dave to take any chances. "Be careful. It might be playing possum."

Dave assumed his normal tone. "Even possums don't play possum this good. I pretty sure it's dead."

Dave walked back towards the deer trail and then up a way. While the walkie-talkie was more reliable out beneath the trees and up in the hills where the cell phone signal was often lost, there was still something psychological about being able to see some slice of the sky.

"What do you have?" Came back the sheriff's voice.

"One of those things," said Dave, barely able to contain his excitement. "It's as dead as a doornail. Must be the one Aloise shot."

HUNGRY

It was a reflex. "Are you sure it's dead?"

"Yeah, Dad. I'm sure it's dead. Big Red and Swan are both with it right now. It even smells like it's dead. Man, you got to see this thing."

"Okay. Stay with it. We're on our way. And don't touch it."

Dave then heard his father hit up Jeremy and Kenny. He told them to keep up the search on their end, and to get back to him if they found anything. He warned them to be careful. "We now know for sure," he said, "that something is up here."

Eric had gone back down the hill and was waiting when Sheriff Hardy showed up with Matt Dell.

Hardy pulled the *300* into the driveway, stopped short of Lisa's Cherokee. The rear door of the Cherokee had been pushed closed by this time, the groceries placed atop the counter in the kitchen and the perishables tossed.

"It's this way, Sheriff," said Eric when the two had made their way over to him. "Big Red's dog found it beneath some overgrowth. Looks like it crawled in there, curled up and died. Smell's something nasty."

"Nobody's touched it, right?"

Eric shook his head. "Not without gloves. That thing stinks worse than skunk. You get that shit on your hands, who knows if it'll ever come off."

"What's it look like?" Asked Dell as they made their way up through the trees, Eric taking the lead.

Eric looked back over his shoulder. "It doesn't look to be all that big. Has some kind of hair or fur all over its body, but short and tight. Can't be sure about the color. I'd say maybe a hay color, something like that—maybe like a lion. But it's hard to tell the way it's curled up in there. The hair kind of catches the surrounding greens and browns of the tree and leaves. Almost like a reflection. The way it's in there, you can't see the face too good. It's facing away, into the hollow."

"It's an animal?" Asked Dell, the sheriff content to listen.

"I guess so," said Eric, his tone not convinced. "Like I said, it's hard to get a good look at it. But if it's a person, it ain't like any person I've ever seen. I mean, it's not wearing any clothes or nothing like that. It's got its back to the opening, so you can see its legs and all. The rump, the way it's curled up in there, looks kind of human, if you don't count the hair. I didn't see any tail. And the legs, too; you know, the way they're shaped. At least what you can see. It just looks small, is all. Like a kid, but not a little kid. Thin like one but taller, longer-limbed."

"How much further?" The sheriff wanted to know, his breath coming with greater effort than he would have liked. He blamed it on the humidity.

Eric used his head to indicate. "About another hundred yards. To the left there. It's a tree that must have gone down in a storm some time ago. It's overgrown and with a hollow formed where the roots came up and the trunk went down."

When they reached the spot, Big Red had Sheba leashed, and she was sitting calmly by his side. Dave was using his cell phone camera to get some photos. He included the hollow from every angle, and also got shots of the surroundings, including the ground along which the thing had dragged itself.

The sheriff nodded when he saw the camera. "Good idea. I should have thought to bring the one from the car." He thought about sending Eric back to get it. Decided he'd get all the pictures he needed later, once they got it down the Hill.

Instead, he moved over to the spot and crouched down. The thing was deep enough in there that he had to go down on one knee so as to be able to lean forward and get a good luck. It was pretty much as Eric had described it, especially the part about catching and reflecting the color. But he could tell also that it was definitely a tawny color, if not a tad bit more on the yellow side.

"Holy shit, this thing does reek. It's worse than what Bob had described. And I don't know what to call it. It's not really that dead and decaying smell, but more like some kind of horny musk. Wow."

He moved back from the hollow and got back to his feet. "We're going to have to get it out of there and get it back to the office, or better yet, over to Dr. Dave." He turned to Dave and Eric. "What's the chance you guys got a tarp or blanket in the unit?"

Dave shook his head. "Not that I know of."

Hardy turned to Big Red. "Can we throw it in the back of your bed?"

Big Red already had a smirk across his face. "I'd have to spend the rest of the day hosing it down. Forget that."

Eric pointed in the direction of the White's house. "I'm pretty sure we left the front door unlocked. I can run down there and pull off a bed spread, or see if Dr. White has some extra sheets."

Hardy hesitated only for a moment. He nodded. "And bring up the box of rubber gloves." He tossed Eric the smart key to the *300*. "They're in the trunk."

HUNGRY

Robert Hardy, PhD

The restaurant was a small place not too far from the university. The food was good, the prices reasonable, and it was far enough to not have to be concerned with running into students. The tables were to the back of the place and the lighting low. And none of the wait staff were students. The place was family own and operated, the food Mediterranean.

Robert Hardy checked his watch. He was early. Joy would be late. That was her MO. But always just fashionably so. As for going with him up to the Valley, he was sure she would say yes. First, because she loved getting away, the two of them, when the opportunity arose. Two, because she was a zoologist, and there was no way she was going to pass up a chance to examine whatever this creature was that his dad couldn't identify.

He had plans to leave right away. Have a nice meal, and then get on the road. He made that as clear as possible in his text to Joy: Pack light, he had said. We'll be gone for the weekend. He knew she would know what he meant.

Dr. Hardy had not been back to the Valley since Christmas. His work at the university kept him busy, whether it was teaching, writing, lecturing, doing book engagements or even traveling. In fact, he had just gotten back from spending a month in the jungles of Central America, living among different indigenous people, which if no longer actually tribal in the sense that they were running around the jungle naked, still held to most of their traditional ways, including foregoing most of what the modern world had to offer. Not that it mattered. Dr. Hardy was more interested in the places they could lead him to, and what it was he could discover once there. He had enough for another book and for a series of short lectures—all of which helped pay the bills.

Dr. Hardy left the Valley almost immediately after earning his undergraduate degree. Laughing to himself, he recalled his own days as a busboy, a waiter, and then as a bartender, serving drinks to under-aged college students with really bad phony ID. But then again, the local authorities rarely checked, and when they did, somehow word always got out that they were coming. After all, college towns get by on what the college kids spend. If you chase them away from the local watering holes, then there would be no local watering holes. And everybody knows, if you want to keep the flow going, you've got to keep the watering holes full.

Of course, his father had wanted him to join the valley police department. Even went so far as to promise him a new SUV. That's what every high school boy in the Valley dreamed about: wearing a deputy's uniform and driving one of the vehicles with the big insignia on the door.

But not him. He wanted to get away from the Valley, go out and see more of the world. And it wasn't a negative thing. He had no inhibitions about being Native American, and no qualms about being from the reservation. In fact, most people he knew, and that knew him, whether it was as a little kid, or later in high school, or even these days, fully realized the Valley was a reservation.

"Not for me, Dad," he had said. "I really want to see how far I can take this anthropology thing."

He wasn't sure how much his father got it, but Sheriff Hardy was a bright man. "Can you make a living out of that kind of thing?" He had asked.

Robert had smiled. "It's a world of its own," he said. "None of it much matters in the world at large, but within its circles, yeah, I can make a living. Of course, I'll have to teach, do some writing, and hopefully become interesting enough to do some speaking engagements, lectures, things like that. I won't get rich, but it'll pay the bills."

Whatever he had said, the sheriff was behind him one-hundred percent, helping Robert take out the loans he needed; all of which had been long since repaid.

Robert was kind of surprised to get the text. It was unusual for his father to reach out. Usually it was the other way around, and even then, not as frequent as it should have been. This text started out as all the others, a 'Hello, how are you?" But then it had appended to it, 'give me a call.' And that was enough to mean today, now.

Once they had moved passed the small talk, and Robert was sure to ask how his mother was doing, the rest of the family and friends, it was the sheriff who got to the point, first filling his son in on the killings, and then describing what they found. He left no open for Robert to express his condolences, or to get on to more details. Robert let it go, knowing there'd be time for all of that once he was in the Valley. Priorities—that was his father's way.

"Nothing like I've ever seen before," the sheriff said. He then went on to describe it, adding before Robert could make the suggestion, "I just sent you some photos. Let me know if you got them."

Robert opened the first one, then the second and third. There was no conversation between his father and him while he took a look. Robert then said, "You're not playing some kind of gag on me, are you Dad?"

"You know me better than that."

And Robert did. He knew what the answer would be before he even asked. But looking at what he was looking at, he had to entertain the obvious first.

127

HUNGRY

"I've never seen anything like it," was all he could think to say.

"We're sure there's more of them, up in the hills, probably back up on the grounds. We're on our way up there to take a look."

Robert was well aware that by *the grounds* his father meant the burial grounds, a part of the hills and woods, which despite the modernization of the valley and the adaptation of the reservation folk to the day's technological society, still held enough taboo and superstition to keep people away. Regardless of how civilized things had become, there was still the lingering notion that the spirits of the dead haunted that place. Some of the older folks remained convinced there were portals up there through which the Holy People would pass to check on this world. Or worse, that there were shadow walkers who would cross over to feed on the life force of the living, if they could lure you into one of the many barrows hidden beneath the brush or behind the breaks of stone.

He recalled being part of the local dare, one side or the other, to go up there every Halloween, and then later as they got older together, to smoke pot or share a beer with the spirits. He could honestly say that nothing had ever happened, but at the same time, he wasn't ready to deny that there was something deeply spiritual about the place, or say with any conviction that there wasn't any kind of supernatural or paranormal entity in some way present, perhaps just a lingering sense of being or a watchfulness.

Looking back on those days now, and with a much more experienced and varied perspective, he was, in fact, convinced there were more possibilities in this world than impossibilities. After all, when a belief or conviction touches on every culture in the world, and more so, those not based on the concept of inherent good and evil, a corresponding reward in the Hereafter, there must be something to it. But then again, maybe that was just the anthropologist in him.

128

HUNGRY

Robert was pretty sure he knew what his father meant by 'have a look': the sheriff and his deputies were going hunting. "You don't want to wait until we get there? I'd love to catch them alive."

There was a moment of silence. "It's going to get dark soon," came back the response. "Even if you were to leave now, you wouldn't get here before midnight, and that's if you break the speed limit the whole way. From what Dr. Dave can tell me, these things are probably nocturnal. Something to do with the eyes, he said. Hard to tell by the photos I sent, but they've got really big pupils, and by the looks of it, from what the Doc can tell, they don't seem to dilate. Not made for the dark, specifically, but definitely not designed for daylight. At least that's his take on it. Which is why I was hoping you'd bring Joy. Something like this is right up her alley.

"But no, we can't wait. If these things are hungry, they'll be on the hunt again. We've put out a warning to the folks to stay inside and keep their doors and windows shut tight, but I can't have any more killings. We've got to get them first."

Robert acknowledged that he understood. "We'll be there as soon as we can."

Joy had barely sat down at the table and Robert had his cell phone down in front of her, encouraging her to scroll through the photos.

"What is this?" She asked having looked at all three. "Something out of Area 51? One of those ET conventions?"

Robert was biting on his lower lip. Something he did when he was amped up about something. "My dad has this thing in the clinic in the Valley. Apparently, from what he tells me, a number of these things attacked and killed four community members. This one was shot during the attack. It got away a short distance and was found later, crawled up beneath some brush. He wants us to come up there."

Joy had that expression on her face which suggested she wasn't quite sure if Robert was serious. She saw his teeth over his lower lip. "You're not kidding, are you?"

Robert, shaking his head ever so slightly, slid the menu over to her. "We'll have us a nice meal and then hit the road."

"My car or yours?" She asked.

"I'll drive."

"That doesn't answer the question."

Robert waved over the waitress. "That would depend on whether or not you mind leaving your car here in the parking lot."

"You can drive."

Robert smiled. "That doesn't answer the question."

"Yours."

Robert took his eyes off the road to glance over at Joy. She had his cellphone in hand. She had been scrolling back and forth from one photo to the other for the entire hour to that point that they had been driving. "You've given those photos the once over, what, about a hundred times now? So, are you going to share with me what you're thinking?"

Joy returned his glance. "Keep your eyes on the road. Traffic or not, I don't want to wind up in a ditch off the shoulder." She then waited for him to do so before answering the question. "Well, I can't be sure of anything until I actually see it. But I don't see any nipples, and the feet are ungulate but the hands are not."

It was a term Robert hadn't heard a bunch in conversation. "Ungulate? You mean like a camel?"

HUNGRY

"Pigs, deer, elk, rhinos...from what I can see, yes. The one photo's a pretty good close-up. But I can't tell if it's two toes with a retracted third behind, or just the two."

"And that tells us what?"

She enlarged the photo, took a closer look. "Nothing much, really. An adaptation. The creature moves upright, on two legs. Probably has pretty good speed and agility. The length of the arms, the shape and size of the hands—an opposable appendage from what it looks like, suggest dexterity, and believe it or not, says something about the intelligence."

"But it doesn't tell you what it is, by which I mean to say, species or family?"

Joy shook her head, a gesture lost on Robert now that his eyes were where she recommended. "No. I have no idea. But I am fairly confident that there's nothing similar on this planet, feet of an ungulate and human-like hands."

"And the nipple thing?"

"Could suggest it's not a mammal. There are some mammals that don't have them, brown rats, mice, and even male horses. But I can't think of any that are upright like this."

Robert recalled the photos. "And this one's definitely a male."

Joy's voice had a hint of the obvious. "The penis would seem to suggest that, yes."

"That it would."

Joy laughed. "Okay, now your turn, Mr. Anthropologist. What's your take?"

Robert thought to preface his response, but not to editorialize. "Remember, you're talking to a Mohawk, a Native American. Our various cultures have all kinds of references for this type of thing. You've heard of the Jersey Devil, no doubt. The Lenape called those woods down there the place of the dragon. The Algonquin

131

HUNGRY

have the Wendigo—right here in this region. The Ute and Navajo out west have Skinwalkers. There's also the Chupacabra, the rake demon, and the Beast of Bray Road, to name a few. There are shadow walkers, Holy People, and demons and spirits that supposedly cross over into this world through portals and alternate dimensions, different planes. And while I'm not saying that thing in the photo is any of these, what I am saying is that it would not be far-fetched to say all of these myths and cryptids originated from something real. Something someone had actually seen."

Joy fought against the temptation to state the obvious. But as an academic, it needed to be said. "Aren't they generally cannibalism taboos? Eat human flesh and you turn into one of these things?"

"That's a big part of it, yes," Robert acknowledged. "Still, taboos don't account for the creature itself, what it looks like, the physical characteristics. The similarities given the absence of contact one culture to the other, hard to dismiss that."

Joy continued the devil's advocacy. "A combination of the meaner parts of the local wildlife: snout, canines, claws—that kind of thing."

"Granted. But then again, we have these photos. And whatever it is, it's in the clinic there in the Valley, and we're on our way to see it."

Joy sucked back on her lips. "What's the chance we get to see one of these things alive?"

Robert thought about the sheriff and his deputies, each one armed with a hunting rifle. "Depends on how good they are at hiding."

HUNGRY

The Hunt

The alpha stirred from the crook in the rock in which he had nestled to sleep. Stretching his arms and legs, he gathered himself and stood. It took a moment for his eyes to adjust to the dark shades of grey which had replaced the amber to which he was accustomed. Turning his head and moving his eyes from one side to the other, he examined his surroundings, the rock and straggling roots just over his head, the damp earth beneath his feet, and the narrow and descending tunnel sinking back into the darkness.

He wrinkled his nose to take in the air. There was too much of it and it was heavy and damp. He waited for its strangeness to pass, felt the redolence of the other males on his tongue. The scent of the lesser one, the reckless one was missing. It was nothing more than a passing recognition.

Moving deeper into the barrow, he came upon the other males. They stirred at his presence, and one after the other came awake, even the young one. Taking in more of their collective scent, the alpha detected nothing of hunger. They, like he, had had their fill from the earlier hunt.

He left them there in the low-ceiling chamber, up upon their feet, crouched and waiting.

The females were where they had been during the frenetic coupling. Both were tending to the new born, watching as it filled its mouth with small handfuls of brain matter it was pinching from the surface of the stone upon which it squatted. There were four skulls lying discarded against the far wall. The eyes were gone. Most of the facial skin had been peeled away, the hair and scalp, too. Gaps in the skull showed hollow within.

HUNGRY

The alpha moved closer, the new born paying him no heed. Both females, though, eyed him warily, tensed and ready to spring. Were the newborn to appear, in any way, weak or sickly or unwanted, the alpha would kill it. The females, though, would come to its defense, regardless. And they'd fail.

The alpha paused well within arm reach of the newborn. He closed his eyes, turning his head ever so slightly, poking his nose and short muzzle forward. Wrinkling his nose, his nostril widening, he breathed in the newborn's scent, let its musk settle on his tongue. It was a female. He turned and left, showing no other interest.

The alpha knew, too, by the musk of both females that the previous night's coupling had succeeded. It mattered not to him whether it was him or one of the others. The survival of the clan was all that mattered.

He made his way back to where the other males were waiting. The young one was among them. But the alpha curled back his lips, bared his teeth when he attempted to follow.

The young one would not be so easily cowed. Instead, he stepped closer to the other three males, sought to conceal himself behind their numbers, and pressed forward.

The alpha held his ground, lips still curled, teeth still bared, but this time a low, guttural hiss rolled from his throat.

It was enough to part the other three males. They moved away from the young one, left him exposed to the glare of the alpha.

The young one gave up and slinked back down the tunnel of the barrow. But there was no turning his back to the alpha. He fixed his gaze, his eyes hard and unflinching. He had been thwarted this time, but not the next.

The alpha waited until the young one had retreated all the way back toward the females. He could smell their proximity. He then turned and made his way out into the darkness of the night. The other three males followed.

Once outside into the night air, the alpha led the clan males across the length of the hill top. Moving cautiously, he kept to the long stretches of rock poking up through the ground and huddled together like wide, flat altars. Here and there, wherever a hold cold be found, random mats of velvety moss, grasses and stubborn scrub grew upon the surface, pushed out of weatherworn cracks and crevices. To the far side of the rock, the tree line took up again, running long to the west and circling around to the south.

It didn't matter what might be deeper into the trees or beyond. To the alpha, here was the first boundary to their new territory.

He sniffed at the air, tasting alien smells in his mouth. But there was no scent that matched that of the predators from which they had been fleeing. To be sure, he leaped atop the nearest rock, used it as a step and vaulted effortlessly to a point higher up. As he did so, the other three males moved off a short distance, each in a different direction, to spray the surrounding trees and stone with their urine. It was the clan way of marking territory, so that no other clan might mistakenly approach.

Detecting nothing of danger, the alpha jumped back down to ground level, the three males falling in at his back. Across the hill and down they moved, stopping here and there to leave their scent, always the three subordinate males urinating while the alpha watched and waited.

As they broke the tree line along Sylvan Road, the alpha paused. Here his head was suddenly flooded with a wash of brightness. He squeezed his eyes tight against the piercing pain he anticipated, but it didn't come, the headlights of the passing car nowhere near as insistent as the yellow fire in the daytime sky. Far enough from the shoulder of the road to go unnoticed, the alpha waited until the red of the taillights dwindled and disappeared before leading the others out upon the pavement.

No sooner had they gained the far side of the road the alpha caught the scent of the lesser male. It was feint and fading and smelled of blood. He stopped, stood still and listened. He snuffled the air and stuck his tongue out to taste it. There was nothing. Quickly, sensing the danger of remaining exposed out in the open, he pushed into the trees and the others followed.

Here the ground sloped at a lesser angle, the alpha leading them through a swathe of sugar maples, oaks, and cypress not much wider than a football field is long. There were branches reaching out just above their heads, dwarf firs and other brush to tangle their feet. The alpha found and stuck to a well-worn deer trail, pausing frequently for the other males to spray as they went along.

Soon he led them to a place where the trees ended and the space before them opened up. Here about were caves-not-a-cave, each decorated with rectangular patches of glaring brightness— windows lit by the lamps within. The light wasn't strong enough to bring on that ache behind the eyes, but was enough to make them look away.

So as not to move directly towards the light, the alpha led them around. They stuck to the tree line, making for the back of the houses where the glare was comparatively pale and the darkness concealed their approach. The other males marked each foundation in a different way, one that suggested a food source, a place of prey.

But this night was not a hunting night. Not wanting to betray their presence, the alpha moved off quickly, and the others followed.

HUNGRY

As many times as there were houses, the alpha moved in circles using the darkness to approach, then waiting while each was marked. Three times he brought the clan's males to spots in which their own scent still lingered heavily and in which that of prey elicited false pangs of hunger, short-lived but imprinting.

At the last of those spots, the alpha caught a stronger, fresher scent of the lesser male. It filled his head with his image, vague and removed as it was. Following it, he led the others back towards the trees and away from the driveway in which Lisa's Cherokee remained parked. There past a tree marked with a length of yellow ribbon, he stepped onto the deer trail and started upward. Here the smell was strong, and it pulled him along.

As he climbed, the other three in his wake, he detected a mix of other scents, too. They were many and alien, and among them one in particular which sought his attention. It was distinct, more feral, more primal. It had the edge of a predator...but not enough to deter him from the path.

Up a way, the alpha left the deer trail and navigated the tangles at his feet, small thorns grabbing at his lower leg, but finding no hold. He ignored them other than to acknowledge the annoyance. Within a few strides he came upon the felled tree and the tall, earth-packed roots. The scent of the lesser male was strong there but without its fullness. It stank, too, of death. The alpha was familiar with the taste.

The alpha turned from the spot, feeling no need to linger. The others, still at his back, had come no further, felt no need to mark the spot or otherwise pay it any heed.

Up the deer trail the alpha led. The tree line ended, and again they were on the shoulder of Sylvan road. The way back to the lair lay before them.

HUNGRY

But the alpha froze. There was a new scent. It was suddenly heavy in his nostrils and pasted on his narrow tongue. He stuck the tip of it out slightly from his thin lips. Let more of the scent settle. It was feral and strong, not much different than the one he detected back by the fallen tree, where the lesser one died. Only this scent was stronger, and after a few sniffs, clearly from multiple sources, each individually distinct from the other—much in the same way he distinguished one clan member from the other.

The coyotes, three of them—the biggest, a male, out front, trotted casually out from the trees to the far side of Sylvan road. Suddenly, as if he caught the musk of the clan members, the big male stopped and lifted his nose to the air. With hesitation, he stepped one paw on the road surface, and again grew still. The other two coyotes remained back on the grassy surface, prepared to at any moment take for the cover of the trees.

The alpha remained still as the strange clan came into view. Then raising his head ever so slightly, he drew in the scent. He recognized of it neither prey nor predator.

By instinct, the other clan males moved off, noiselessly working into an attack position around the three new-comers, one to each side, and the third circling in behind them.

To distract the members of this strange clan and to allow his own to get in position, the alpha stepped out from beneath the trees and revealed himself. Immediately, he started taking strides directly toward the alpha coyote. By learned instinct, he led with his left foot while dragging the right, feigning injury and appearing vulnerable.

Not yet interpreting any threat, the alpha coyote sat back on his haunches as the alpha male approached. The other two coyotes, however, remained poised, either to flee or attack.

HUNGRY

The alpha stepped into the road, continuing his path toward the coyotes. His hands he held low to his side, revealing his midsection and groin—an inviting distraction. Drawing his lips back, he tasted the air, first to one side and then the other. The three from his clan were in position.

As the alpha reached the middle of the road, the alpha coyote rose back up to full stature. His snout wrinkling against the pungent and unfamiliar musk and the hair at the back of his neck standing, he now arched his back up in warning, his lips drawn back, his fangs bared and a low snarl rolling from his throat. The other two coyotes started to yip and chatter.

The alpha moved forward undeterred.

Just then, a sudden explosion of fiery brightness flared from deep in the darkness. It came from behind the coyotes and up the hill. It washed across the alpha's eyes, momentarily blinding him. Instinctively, he crouched low to the ground, his arms and hands raised as if to meet an on-rush. At the same, a sharp crack came out from beneath the trees, repeating itself over and over as it faded down into the valley.

Having experienced before the sound of the rifle shot, the coyotes scattered, the male turning back towards the trees and immediately veering to his left, the other two following in his steps.

The alpha, his senses returned, was back to his feet. The musk of the clan male farthest from him suddenly punched at him with a dense air of panic and distress. The alpha experienced the moment of that one's death by a sudden and near-disorienting spin that almost took his feet out from beneath him. And then just as quickly, the feeling was gone.

Knowing he was in danger, the alpha darted across the road back in the direction from which they had come and sought cover beneath the branches of the trees. The two remaining males reappeared out of the trees on the opposite side, the scent of flight strong about them. And there were other scents, too, carried by the night stir and narrowing the alpha's vision.

Again, a sudden and violent wash of light flared out of the dark woods in front of him, less bright, less intense, but more encompassing. It blinded his eyes and stabbed into his head. Then came a series flashes, more violent, more intense—brief bursts of fire burning away the black of night. Gun shots, then more gun shots. A volley. With tunnels of pain burrowing into his brain, the alpha he went to his knees. A brief moment of silence followed. The guns then reloaded, there was a sporadic shot fired, then another. The barks cascaded their way down the hillside, echoed out across the valley and faded.

The night again dark, the alpha cautiously stood, a wide bole between him and the road. Head tilted upward he sniffed at the humid air for the two remaining males. He found only one. He came out from behind the tree and moved back across Sylvan Road, taking to the same path upon which the coyotes had fled. No sooner did he start uphill, he stumbled upon the last remaining male. Shot, he was holding his hand pressed tight to his chest, the blood soaking thick from beneath his fingers and leaking unchecked down the fine hair carpeting his mid-section.

The alpha drew back his lips, his mouth opening, and tasted the lingering air. Thin and fading, the scent of the two males already killed settled upon his tongue. He wrinkled his nose one more time, let slip a muted growl. Aware of from which direction the danger lay, he turned and once again headed downhill towards the road. He gave no glance over his shoulder to see if the wounded male would follow. It didn't matter: the wound was fatal. There was also no ignoring that their prey had now turned predator, and it was he who was being hunted. Their stink was strong and coming at him from behind and ahead.

He'd go down and not up. Not to escape, but to lead the hunters away from the two females, the young male and the new born. Whether he survived wasn't part of the process.

There was no sticking to the deer trail on the way down. There were predators there, coming up towards him. Hesitating but for a second, the alpha turned to his right and started jogging, following Sylvan Road as it ran east to turn north. He saw only the peripheral flashes of the light as they were reflected by the waxy leaves up in the tree tops in front of him. Multiple rifle shots cracked against the rocks and echoed. A bullet punched him to the outside of his left shoulder, but not enough to spin him or stop him. The shoulder began to burn.

Moving with long, fluid strides, the alpha quickly outpaced the pursuit of the predators. This time crossing the road, he disappeared into the trees of the lower hill, started moving down. There were sounds to his back which were alien. They were like the bark of predators he knew but evoked no clear image.

It was then that he sensed pursuit of a different kind, a distinct smell apart. It was more primal, more feral. It brought to him no urge to quicken his pace but heightened his need for caution. He kept to his jog but zigged and zagged, keen for fallen trees to leap or patches of briars to cut through. Delay the inevitable, that was his intent, to put more distance between him and the the lair, from the two females, the young male and the new born.

Down he went into a bowl of twisted vine and thick grass, the heavy humidity in the air taking its toll, pressing upon his chest. He shook his head to clear away a distracting eddy of dizziness.

Almost too late.

HUNGRY

Spartacus came hurtling down the hill. Cutting first around one tree and then another, the black Lab launched itself from a distance just up slope from the alpha.

Suddenly aware of the danger, the alpha turned. The weight of the black lab crashed into his left side, teeth slashing just below his arm. But the alpha was quick. He brought his elbow down sharp upon the top of the dog's head.

It was a solid shot which drove the dog straight to the ground.

Surprised, Spartacus failed to find footing, landing on his side and sliding a short distance downhill where the dog's front paws were tangled by vines and he was catapulted nose first into covered rock with a thud and a yelp.

Before the dog could regather its footing, the alpha sprung. Well-practiced in the hunt, he slashed out with the long fingers and rigid nails of his right hand, grasping the dog at the throat. With a savage tug, a fistful and more of flesh and sinew came away. Spartacus' eyes widened with confusion and then the life went out of them. There was a single twitch and the dog went still.

The alpha crouched low to the ground, using the trees and the darkness to conceal his location, taking a moment to catch his breath, for the throbbing pain at his shoulder to subside.

Raising and tilting his nose to the breeze pushing at the leaves over his head, the alpha knew the proximity of the hunters. He caught, too, the scent of Big Red's second dog, Sheba. He knew by that scent that it was a female, and that she lacked the fierceness of the one that lie dead at his feet.

Unhurried, the alpha raised the flesh from Spartacus' throat to his nose. He sniffed at its warmth before licking at the blood with the tip of his tongue. Satisfied, he carved the bits of meat from the hair and skin with his teeth. Discarding the rest to the ground, he rose to his feet and sniffed the air. Sensing the hunters' approach

HUNGRY

near, he started down the hill, his long steady strides extending the distance between them but only enough to lead them on, not elude.

Sheba, secured by a leash, pulled Jeremy along, strong on the spore of the animal, its musk eliciting a steady whine from her as she moved him onward to the tree line.

The alpha was immediately aware of the open-space now looming before him. He halted just beneath the branches extending above his head. The pursuit was nearer. He turned his head only long enough to smell how near. He then looked again out ahead of him, saw the pale glare of lighted windows. At this distance, there was no discomfort, no tunnels of piercing pain. He smelled prey, the scent muted and feint. Of no immediate interest, he stepped out from the cover of trees and started to jog for the concealing darkness beyond.

There was a sudden flare of blinding brightness. It bloomed out of the darkness before the alpha, the warning cracks of the rifles coming too late. The alpha took both shots like heavy punches, one to his chest and the other to the belly. There was a burning sensation as the bullets tore into him, neither more than an after-thought. Stopped in his steps, the alpha staggered. His faculties no longer his own, he folded down into his knees and then fell face-first into the damp grass, his arms limp at his sides.

Sheba, freed from her leash, came bursting out from the tree line. She charged up to the now fallen alpha, leaping forward and then jumping back, again and again, excited by the chase but confused by the stillness of the catch.

Out of the black, back where Barry Steed's house stood, David Hardy came jogging in the direction of the fallen alpha, the pool of light from his flashlight sliding from the body and then back again.

143

HUNGRY

The barrel of his rifle was pointed to the ground. Trailing in his wake was Big Red Harrison.

"Come, Sheba," he was calling out. "No, girl. Get away, girl."

He had no thought yet for the missing Spartacus.

HUNGRY

God's Good Earth

Katy Hastings moved away from the front window. She thought she heard a car come up, saw the headlights. But it was only someone driving by.

She was awaiting a visit from Father Jacob. He had been making a habit of himself lately, coming by rather frequently, and even at times unannounced.

She understood, though, why he'd want to come this evening. It had been a particularly difficult day for him, what with the services for all four victims of the attacks.

There had been some thought that they'd all be put off, something about conducting investigations, evidence, things like that. But with the news that the animals that had done the killing had been hunted down and they themselves now dead, the sheriff gave Dr. Dave the okay to go ahead and release the remains. No sense denying people their final rest.

Katy cringed at referring to lost tribal members as remains, even if it was in thought only, and to herself, at that. She knew, though, at least from what she had heard, remains were all there were. Hardly more than some meatless bones, odd patches of skin, strands of hair and sneakered feet.

All four wakes were held at the same time—closed caskets, the funerals immediately following. It was agreed upon by all involved. Only the locals were there for Barry Steed. Tanya had told Katy during one of the moments they had aside that she did the best she could to reach out to whatever family of his she could reach. But then having said her part, she was left with the feeling none of them would show. None did. Bob Aloise had his four children gathered around him, and all had gone on their way shortly after

145

the casket was lowered. Then there was Maggie White, the poor girl. Dr. Dave and Gayle had handled the arrangements for her, selecting caskets of good taste for both Lisa and Andy, and seeing to it they were laid to rest beside husband and father. Katy noted, too, how stoic and solid Maggie presented during both wake and funeral, responding with grace to those who expressed condolences and the pain and sadness they couldn't suppress. Word was Maggie would be moving in with Dr. Dave and his wife before the weekend was out.

The cemetery was to the northwest extent of the Valley, a garden-like plot of land isolated at the base of the hills, surrounded by tall trees, and at the end of a narrow winding road which passed in through the iron-wrought gate and ran in a full-circle about the inner-perimeter. There were foot paths paved with block neatly arranged about the headstones.

Katy had made sure to spend an equal amount of time with each of the mourners, and then following the last of the services, she had taken the rest of the morning and some part of the early noon to pay her respects to all those who rested there, chanting in a low voice the words her mother and father had taught her, and to them their parents before. She was at peace, and felt the dead were, too.

After she got back to her own house, she set to the task of readying the items she would need to help Barry, Darla, Lisa, and Andy find their way to that place where the living must journey once their time on Earth has ended.

Certainly, she was Christian, as were Barry, Darla, Lisa and Andy. As Christians, they held to the faith of the here-after and the Holy Father. But being faithful didn't mean abandoning the way things have always been, and always will. Souls or spirits or ghosts, interpret it any way you like. All that live must die, but when it came down to it, all Mohawk must return to the beginning by the road of the dead. Only then could the Holy Spirit that decides such things choose to send them back again, or perhaps onto some other plane. As for their Christian souls, God take them where He may.

As the tribal medicine woman, shaman, spiritual leader—the particular title didn't matter, it was Katy's responsibility to assure that the ritual was performed, and performed properly. It was she that made the clay pots. It was she that painted them with the appropriate colors and characters. It was she that filled them with the foodstuffs that would sustain the dead along the road. It was she that made the candles that would light the way. And, ultimately, it was she who would go up into the burial grounds to place both clay pot and lighted candle so that the dead might know the way.

It surprised her, then, that Maggie had approached her among the headstones. At first, the young lady seemed hesitant to speak her mind, leaving Katy to fill the silence with words of condolence and small talk. When there was nothing left to say, the two of them walked together a while, Katy returning to her words to the spirit world and Maggie silent.

But then Maggie surprised Katy, saying, "Ms. Hastings, I want to go with you, up to the top of the hill. I'd like to place the candles myself."

It was not a request often made. Mostly, Katy would go on her own, not tell anyone. When it came to the traditional rites, those in the Valley had come to take for granted that Katy would see to it. It was one of those just-in-case things—just in case there actually was a road of the dead. Better safe then sorry.

Katy knew it was the right thing for Maggie to do. Lisa and Andy would find comfort in Maggie's presence and it would take away much of the fear and anxiety the recently living would feel embarking upon the road of the dead.

"Are you sure?" Katy asked.

Maggie nodded. "I have to."

"Come by tomorrow just before sundown," Katy told her with a smile. "And bring with you something small that belongs to your mother and something from your brother. An earring from mom, perhaps. For your brother—well, I'm not sure. Something he'd recognize as his, something I can put in the jar. In this way, they'll know the jars are there for them. Then we'll light the candles as night falls and they'll know the way."

Katy Hastings had come to the conclusion that Father Jacob counted her as a sort of confidant, someone he could talk to in matters of faith.

At first, she had the impression that he saw her as some source of conflict, a heathen soul which he was obligated to save and convert. But as she was a Sunday mass regular, he soon gave up on the conversion part. The heathen soul, however, she felt he had a need to hold onto, if only because it gave him that small part of contrast which he used to keep his own conviction in perspective.

Katy found that part of it very interesting, that a priest's faith would hinge on so tenuous a thread.

It didn't take long, however, from their conversations, most of which took place on weekday evenings, and always over tea and then brandy, that Father Jacob's conflicts with his faith were a much deeper thing. Eventually, and these many years later, he confided in her that he was unsure how much of what he did was faith and how much was obligation.

Katy saw no wrong in this, and said as much, assuring the good Father that what mattered was the peace of mind and serenity he brought to his parishioners, many of whom came from outside the Valley. "Ultimately," she would tell him, "all will know the truth when the time comes, and none of this will matter."

Father Jacob seemed to take some solace in her words, but at the same time he worried that if things didn't turn out the way he promised—the *Word* promised—that he'd be the one they blamed.

Katy would always smile at that. Then remind him of the Mohawk way. "Could Heaven be any other way?" She would challenge him. "To walk the road of the dead. To go back into the spirit world from which all Earth People come. Then perhaps to come again, none the wiser. What pain and suffering can there be in that?"

Katy sat at the small table in the work room off the kitchen. She was putting the final touches on Andy's jar. It was then that Heidi's pointed ears perked up. Then up came her head. Katy heard it, too. Father Jacob's car was turning up the drive.

The Shepherd-collie mix was already sniffing at the base of the front door when Katy got there to open it. Father Jacob was coming up the walkway. He'd have no need to knock.

"I'd have thought you'd be by earlier," said Katy by way of greeting, the door open and Heidi out on the porch having the top of her head scratched by Father Jacob.

The Father took hold of the door and let Heidi lead him in. "I stopped in to see the sheriff."

It was a response Katy had not expected.

"The sheriff?"

They sat together in the parlor, a small fire burning in the fireplace. There was absolutely no need for the added warmth, but for Katy there was an earthiness to the flames, an earthiness that otherworldly spirits and entities could not abide. It was a tribal thing Father Jacob had come to accept. The teapot, too was on the coffee table, alongside two cups.

"Yes, Sheriff Hardy. He has the bodies of those things in the coroner's lab there at the back of the clinic. There's five of them all together."

"So, you saw them?"

The Father nodded. A short laugh followed which he did not intend. "Seems he wanted a professional opinion."

Katy didn't understand, and said as much.

"He asked me to come back with him into the room, the one where Dr. Dave lays out the recently deceased before he sends them over to the funeral parlor. He had me take a look, and then he actually asked me if there was anything in the scripture, perhaps *Revelation*."

"About what? I don't think I'm following you."

"I'm not sure where to start. They had all five of those things laid out on the steel tables. You know the kind."

Katy shrugged in acknowledgement. "I've been back there a time or two. I've got the idea."

"Well, they're not like anything I've ever seen before. Face-wise, I'm tempted to say canine-like. But not as pronounced. You know, the snout or muzzle, whatever you want to call it. The actual nose is small, and the mouth, too, with only the merest of lips. The eyes have this yellowish color, you know, where ours are white. And they have these large black pupils. But no iris, from what the doc said. Or maybe it was Robert. He was there, too, with a colleague of his from the university."

Katy interrupted. "Rob? Harvey's son."

Father Jacob gave a short nod and went on. "The colleague is a woman."

HUNGRY

"I believe her name is Joy," said Katy. "They've been talking about getting married for some time now, so Harvey says. Haven't made the leap yet."

"So, she's from Cornell, too? Or is it Concordia? I mix those two up."

"I believe it is Cornell."

"Any way, the two of them were there, and there was some talk about doing an autopsy. Apparently—what did you say her name was? Joy? Well, she's a zoologist. They do stuff like that."

"They're definitely animals?"

Father Jacob looked at Katy as if she had already been at the brandy. "What else? They're covered with hair, though it looks to be really fine, tight to the skin. And I'm not sure of the color. Maybe tawny, like lions. It was hard to be sure. Even lying there on those tables, depending on the angle and the lighting, the exact color seemed to change." He then raised his hand up well above his head, and his palm to the ground. But as he was seated, the height wasn't all that much. "That's about how tall they looked to be, and kind of skinny. But you could tell by looking at them that they're strong, kind of like when you look at a stag or a deer. They might not look all that dangerous, but you don't want one running into you or catching you with a kick."

Katy listened but wasn't yet convinced. "You yourself said they're not like anything you've ever seen. So how can you be sure they're animals?"

"What then, aliens?"

Katy's expression didn't change. "Rumor is they came down from the hill."

Father Jacob had an idea where this was going. "You think they're spirits?"

Katy smiled. It was one of patience. "Not if they were shot to death."

"Then what, demons?"

Again patience, this time in her tone. "Demons, spirits, ghosts, angels…I don't think there's any difference, other than their intent or purpose, if there was to be one. Regardless, these are ethereal entities, apparitions. Obviously, the creatures or beings they have there on those tables are quite corporeal."

Father Jacob took a moment before responding, thinking for something rational to say, something that wouldn't contradict his role or position. "Some type of mutant, maybe." He could only make himself sound half-convinced.

"Maybe, but mutated from what? From coyotes? From wolves? From bears? From us?"

Father Jacob decided he'd not be drawn any further into the conversation. The implications were far more than he was ready to contemplate. The only creatures on God's good Earth were the ones He created. Anything else would raise questions he wasn't prepared to deal with. Unless, of course, we were to blame—man. Ugly? Yes. But it would alleviate those other implications. An abomination, but one for which God himself would eventually exact payment, *Revelation* or no.

"You wouldn't happen to have some of that brandy, would you Katy?"

There was no more tea that evening.

HUNGRY

A Closer Look

The alpha had been stretched out on an examining table. His chest cavity remained open, the skin peeled back to each side, the sternum sawed down the middle and the ribs parted. His heart had been fully resected and placed in a stainless-steel dish which had been placed on ice under glass nearby. Joy had also removed his stomach, his liver, both his lungs, and had gone through his back for one of his kidneys—all with the assistance of Dr. Dave. These organs, too, were in their appropriate dish and under glass.

Currently, she was running a circular saw around the circumference of his skull, the skin already peeled back and the face rolled down to the neck.

The process with the saw blade complete, she removed the bone of the skull like a cap and placed it carefully aside. With equal care, she set to removing the alpha's brain, which was done with little effort. It was a process she had done many times before with all kinds of different animals. It, too, went into the appropriate receptacle.

While Joy was performing the cranial procedure, Dr. Dave was involved removing one of the alpha's eyes. He then went to work below the abdomen, opening up the male, and eventually removing one of the testicles. His final task was to open up the thigh to access the muscle and bone structure for comparison not only with humans but with other animals.

The resection complete, Joy began the formal examination, discussing her observations with Dr. Dave and recording both of their comments with her cellphone.

153

HUNGRY

They started with the brain, which Joy stated had a greater ratio to overall weight than that of a chimpanzee, but only by a small percentage, and less than that of the average man.

"So, theoretically more intelligent than the chimp?" Dr. Dave offered.

Joy nodded with agreement. "I would say so. In addition, the area of the cerebral cortex seems greater."

"Reasoning?"

Again, Joy nodded. "Reasoning and memory, among other things. It suggests more complex cognitive function."

"Language?"

"It is the same area of the brain, of course. But really no way of knowing just by looking. But then again, it is readily accepted, and for good reason, that most animal species, if not all, communicate by sound. So, it may not be as developed, but still language."

"What do you make of the eyes?" Asked Dr. Dave, pointing with the pen he had in hand. "Definitely for me one of the more curious aspects of these creatures."

"Most species have very little sclera visible. That these creatures are similar may suggest they are from a predatory environment. There is a benefit when fleeing predators. For example, not giving away with the position of the iris in which direction you are thinking about fleeing.

"As for the size of the pupil, and the yellowish color to what sclera you see, I would think a monochromatic environment. I know how farfetched that might sound on the surface. But given the size of the iris—the pupil—and the absence of dilation, it seems that light refraction, and brightness for that matter, is not something to which they've adapted."

Dr. Dave was pinching his lower lip between index finger and thumb. "Subterranean?"

154

HUNGRY

Dr. Joy shook her head. "I don't think so. For one, too big, and too many of them living in a group. What would they feed upon in quantity enough to meet their needs? Certainly not insects. Look at the teeth: canines and molars. They're primarily carnivores." She realized the obviousness of her statement, and immediately apologized.

Dr. Dave waved it off. "I know what you meant."

"All the same," she said. "I should have been more sensitive."

Dr. Dave moved them past it. "So, the eyes then are not a darkness adaptation?"

"Not darkness. They are adapted to light, but not much of it, and my guess is not with the same spectrum or prism we have here. Going by the other variables available to us, and again this is just an educated guess, I would say shades of amber, something along those lines."

"The sclera?"

Joy shrugged. "That, maybe, but more so the body hair. In this light, it has that tawny kind of shade lions have, or mountain lions. But see how short it is, how tight to the body, almost suede-like. And look at the tip of each hair. It kind of reminds of those fiber optic Christmas trees, where they light up just at the tip. These have an interesting reflective quality to them, a sort of built-in camouflage mechanism. I could see how they might be difficult to distinguish against a background, and especially at a distance."

"Anything like that you know of in terms of species around these parts?"

Joy pressed her lips together, ran her eyes the length of the alpha. "Lots of animals blend in with their environment. White snow rabbits, for example. Wouldn't do much good for one to be brown or black on a white background. Zebras' stripes serve to break them up, as it were. But I'm not telling you anything you

155

don't already know. But something like this? No, not that I can think of offhand."

Dr. Dave wrinkled his brow. "I'm looking for some kind of confirmation here, but I'm not finding it."

Joy gestured towards the dish with the lungs. "Those don't help any. Look at the size and composition. I know you brought this up earlier. I tend to agree. From the looks of them, I'd say designed to be efficient in a low oxygen environment, one in which oxygen is the primary component of the atmosphere, but just where there isn't much of it. So, the lungs are wide and thin to make a little go a long way. I'm not sure what that means exactly in our atmosphere. Less breaths? Smaller ones? I don't know."

Dr. Dave agreed. "With regard to function, I'm not sure it would matter. If anything, just less work. Or maybe even a temporary oxygen high, as it were. That said, we seem to be moving towards some conclusion."

Joy walked down the length of the examining table upon which the alpha lie. She stopped at his midsection. "Before we go doing that, did you happen to notice anything of interest while you were dissecting the sexual organs?"

Dr. Dave was sure that Joy wouldn't be asking if there hadn't been something to notice. He did a quick mental check. Decided he must have missed whatever it was, and said as much.

"It's not something you would have thought to look for. But there is some inflammation to both the vas deferens and the epididymis structure. There is also the presence of ejaculate. Anyway, it suggests recent copulation, I imagine."

Dr. Dave raised his eyebrows. "Unless I missed something, all we have here are males."

Joy bit at her lower lip, stood motionless. She then picked up a scalpel. "I'm curious," she said as she moved to the other examination tables. Indicating the creature upon the furthest table, she said, "You wouldn't mind, would you?"

Dr. Dave shrugged. "What am I looking for?"

"The same thing we have here."

The procedure didn't take long, and the findings were consistent with all four males which were brought in today, but not with the one discovered earlier.

"Unless they're all gay," said Dr. Dave, "it would seem there are females nearby."

Joy nodded. "At least one."

"But probably more."

"No way to tell. Not enough to go on."

Dr. Dave moved away from the examining table he stood beside and back towards the collection of organs. "I should let the sheriff know. Is there anything else I should tell him?"

"About?"

"What it is we're dealing with here."

"What do you suggest?"

"You're the zoologist."

Joy stepped away from the alpha. She removed the rubber gloves she wore. Went over and stopped the phone from recording. "You know," she said, stating what was from her perspective the obvious. "These things are not from here. There's nothing on Earth that looks like this, and nothing to compare. Except for some distant exceptions, and these primarily pre-historic, I don't know of any beast or critter which doesn't share similarities when examining the pairing of feet and hands. Either it's fingers and toes, or it's hooves and hooves, or it's talons and wings. Tentacles if you're an octopus; symmetrical appendages if you're a starfish. I can't think of anything I've ever seen that has ungulate feet and fingered hands.

HUNGRY

"Give a thought to the kinds of animals we have in these parts. Go with the mammals: fox, coyote, bear, the occasional mountain lion, squirrels, raccoons, possums, chipmunks, and the odd wolf. I think you get my drift. Paws. It's all about paws. Why? Because it's the best way to get around, what with the relatively firm soil, grasses, underbrush, and maybe a patch of rock or stone, trees to climb. But ungulate feet—and upon an upright beast—and hands with fingers and opposable thumbs? It's not like we're dealing with Minotaur and centaurs."

Dr. Dave gave a short laugh. "I don't think Hardy will go with either of those."

"I think," Joy took a chance, "you keep it simple. Tell him our findings are inconclusive at the moment. I want to talk with Robert. He's been a lot of places I haven't, and he's seen some strange things. Until then, I think it might be best to stress to the sheriff that there are more of these things still up there. I would suggest they've found a lair, someplace out of the light of the day. And while they are not necessarily nocturnal, I would think they'd stay put while the sun was bright, come out once it's gone down. Are there caves around here?"

Dr. Dave went over towards the sink, peeling his gloves away. "Nothing all that big. But there are other places, especially up by the burial grounds. Lots of rock up there. Some old tunnels." He let the water run.

HUNGRY

There's Going to be Coyotes

Maggie's day did not start off as planned. The way she had it mapped out, she was going to go over to the house with Carly and Monica, and together they were going to pack up her things and take them to Dr. Dave and Gayle's house. Then she was going to get herself settled in her new surroundings, and after dinner head over towards Katy Hasting's place so that they could go up into the hill. Carly said she would go to, and that was alright with Maggie.

Maggie, though, was still not totally sold on the idea of going to live with Dr. Dave and Gayle. They were great people, and as close to family as she had in the Valley. But they never had children of their own, and Maggie was afraid, perhaps, that the everyday reality of having a teenager in their house might wear thin after the initial honeymoon period. Monica told her she could stay with them, and Carly was kind of pushing the matter. There was an extra room in the house, so space wasn't an issue.

But Carly was her best friend, not her sister. There were things you'd tolerate from a sister that just wouldn't be the same with a best friend, and the other way around, too. You could get really mad at a sister—or a younger brother, and it wouldn't make any difference. They'd still be your sister or younger brother. Your mom would see to that.

But if you got mad at your best friend...well, it was just different. You could just avoid them for a couple of days and wait for things to kind of settle themselves. There wouldn't be any need for mom to step in, or to tell you you're acting like children. What would Monica do? Go against her own daughter?

HuNGRY

So, after weighing one against the other, Maggie made her decision based on common sense. Dr. Dave and Gayle had a big house. She'd have her own room up on the second floor, with an on-room suite. All the privacy she needed. Besides, it wouldn't be long before she'd be going away to college, and then when she graduated, she'd have the house.

Then just before Monica was ready to drive them over to the house, the first time that Maggie would be back there since it happened, Father Jacob was on the porch, knocking on the door.

He said he was there to see Maggie, saying to Monica that he thought he would drop by and see how Maggie was doing. He explained how he was left with some concerns following their previous conversation, and now that he had some time to give it proper thought, he thought maybe he and Maggie should try again.

Monica, of course, asked Father Jacob in. She then went over to the stairs and called up to Maggie.

Maggie had no problem with it. She liked Father Jacob. Like just about every other family in the valley, she and Andy and their mother were Sunday regulars. Father Jacob always put on a pretty good show, hitting all the important points when it came to conducting mass and giving sermons, but at the same time, getting the Sunday theme across without sounding preachy or making vague references to the same Good Book quotations and clichés. Besides, it was a great place to see the guys from school wearing something other than the stuff they usually wore. There was something to be said for tucked in shirts, after all.

She came down the stairs and greeted the Father with a genuine smile. They fist-bumped. It was a gesture lost on some adults, but Father Jacob seemed to have it down just right. He even looked comfortable doing it. The Father then asked Monica and Carly if he and Maggie could have some time alone.

160

HUNGRY

Monica took Carly by an empty belt loop on the side of her shorts and pulled her in the direction of the kitchen. "Absolutely, Father. Carly was just going to help me with some kitchen cleanup."

It was a different Maggie that sat with the Father this time.

Three days had passed since her mother and brother had been killed, but for Maggie, it may have been a hundred, or maybe it might not have happened at all. There were moments where everything about them seemed to have moved so quickly into the distance, thinning and fading. Then there'd be moments where she'd have these sudden and vivid images which would pop into her head. Andy would be doing something that annoyed her. Or it would be something that she was sure was uniquely him, but came to her when she saw something similar in another person, for example Carly's brother, Wade. He was only ten, but in some ways like Andy, like all boys. Or perhaps it would be her mother's face, her tone of voice, when Monica would say something to Carly or Wade, like the dinner plates don't take themselves from the table or the lights don't turn themselves off. Mothers, they might all say the same thing, but in the same way, too, and with the same tone?

But Father Jacob told her it was both normal and okay. He called it survival, but made it sound like it wasn't a bad thing, a selfish thing. It's built into us, he said. Otherwise, we wouldn't be able to get out of bed in the morning, given all the bad stuff, the sad stuff that fills our lives in one way or the other. First, we have to come to terms with our new world, the world we now inhabit without our loved ones, without your mother and without Andy. So, our brain gently pushes them into the background. We see them. We know they are there. But we've got to be able to imagine going on without them. Then gradually, as we see the lay of the

161

land that stretches out before us, and without them being part of it, we can let them back in.

He went on to explain it to Maggie as a passive and antagonistic process, in which both extremes gravitate towards the middle. Our loved ones are strong in spirit. They impose themselves whenever they can, their faces, their words, their experiences—the times we've shared—coming to us randomly and unbidden. That's the way it is, he said, until we come to terms with it. Even then, we'll never truly be in control of when or where they choose to drop in on us again.

Consistent with his ways, the very second his words seemed to veer towards insincerity or lecture, Father Jacob changed course. He had the knack for knowing when what needed to be said had been said. The way Maggie put it was that Father Jacob basically said all the same things that every other adult said, or would say, but it just sounded different.

Right there in the middle of being all philosophical, he said, "Katy Hastings told me the two of you are going up the hill tonight."

Maggie measured the Father's tone for any hint of disapproval. It wasn't like traditional lore went hand in hand with Christian doctrine. Remaining neutral, she said, "I thought it was something I might do."

Father Jacob smiled. There was no judgement in it. "Be careful up there."

Maggie saw something in his eyes. "You don't think there's any more of those things, do you?"

"Sheriff Hardy is pretty confident they got them all. But there's regular old coyotes, you know. Katy'll tell you she chased a couple out of her yard only a couple of nights ago."

Maggie shrugged. "They usually stay clear of people, no?"

HUNGRY

It was something the Father had to admit. "Unless you stumble across one of their dens and there are pups. It is that time of year. They'd be a few weeks old, a couple of months even, but the mother coyote will still be protective."

Maggie promised him she would stay away from any coyote dens, confident that Katy would know one if she saw one.

The trip to the house was a short one. Monica had driven Carly and Maggie over. Maggie was somewhat annoyed to find the front door unlocked, and then even more so when she discovered the sheets missing from her mother's bed.

She had made up her mind that having a specific mission would get her into the house, keep out any of those images. So as soon as she stepped through the front door, she made for the stairs, focused on going straight to her mother's room and getting the earring that she had in mind. It was the one remaining from the pair her mother used to wear as her everyday earrings, that was until she lost the other one. She had talked often of finding a replacement for it, but never got around to it.

It was all good. Maggie ignored the blood stains on the floor, hardly noticed the bagged groceries sitting upon the kitchen island, and kept her eyes diverted from the PC and monitor.

Her first thought upon seeing the messed-up bed, the comforter tossed aside, was maybe the sheets were taken for evidence. Mr. Aloise had said something about blood upstairs. But she didn't remember anything about her mother's bed or the sheets.

She almost faltered, then and there. But she caught herself, and went over to the jewelry box on top of the dresser with the big mirror. The earring was right where she knew it would be. It was a simple gold ball with a post. The scent of her mother was there,

163

too. In the bottles gathered like bowling pins there to the side. To the makeup items lined-up according to height to the other. Managing, though, only ghost-like wisps of recall, she didn't let it upset her that she couldn't in the moment remember her mother's face with detail. She thought of Father Jacob had said. It made her feel a little better.

She turned and left the room, back down the stairs, and to Andy's room. She heard Monica and Carly down the hall in her room. Carly knew what Maggie would want packed into the suitcases they had brought along, and what stuff would go in the extra boxes, too.

In Andy's room, she went immediately for his Matt Harvey autographed rookie card, a gold-chrome refractor. The one in the protective plastic shell he kept up on his book shelf. If there was anything that he owned that would get his attention, it was that card. But then Maggie had second thoughts. He'd be pretty upset at her if she put it in a clay jar and left it out where it would be damaged by rain, or whatever, some raccoon coming by and thinking it was worth trying as a snack. He'd never forgive her, going on about the stupid thing like he always did, perfect corners and edges, the surface, and how the card caught the light and showed all those colors. She pictured that expression of his whenever he thought she did something dumb. Unlike her mom's, it came upon her sudden and vivid. He had such beautiful eyes, such perfect features. It made her smile. So instead, she grabbed the *Matchbox* corvette which he kept right beside the card. It was one of the last toys their dad had gotten for him. As for the card, she slipped the case into her pants pocket, deciding on the spot it was something she'd keep until the day she died.

HUNGRY

Carly hadn't said anything about Randy Strongbow. Maggie had assumed that Monica would drive the two of them over to Katy Hasting's house. That's what she had told Dr. Dave and Gayle, right after she asked them if it was alright to go back to Carly's for dinner. It was Carly's idea.

Dr. Dave and Gayle took the request with a bit of hesitation, one exchanging glances with the other. But there was no objection. Dr. Dave had only asked Maggie if she'd be coming home, or had she intended to sleep at Carly's, too.

The 'home' part caught Maggie off guard for a moment. But she recovered quickly. "I was looking forward to getting accustomed to my new bed and room," she responded, and that seemed to put both Dr. Dave and Gayle at ease. Maggie promised she'd be home by 11:00.

Gayle looked at Dr. Dave and gave a little shrug. "I guess that sounds right."

Following dinner, Carly told her mother that she and Maggie were going to go out on the back porch where it was cooler and there was a bit of a breeze. Wade had wanted to come, too. But the expression on Carly's face was enough for Monica to grab him by the wrist and to convince him now was not the time.

It was there, the two of them seated overlooking the line of trees climbing up the hill, that Carly mentioned Randy.

Randy Strongbow was the only kid in the Valley whose family had one of those *Lone Ranger*-type names that the white kids were known to make fun of. But they didn't make fun of Randy. He was his generation's Big Red Harrison, only the high school version, which was a lot more intimidating to kids their age. Not too many six-foot five, two-hundred-thirty-pound high schoolers around, and even less that moved liked Randy did. No one stopped him on the football field; he scored at will for the basketball team; and, he

165

had ultimately decided on accepting that full ride to play baseball at Louisville.

Randy had been showing a keen interest in Carly of late, even though she was a year younger. Maggie thought he was mostly interested in a quick summer romance with all the benefits a boy his age would be fantasizing about when getting up close and personal with a girl as drop-dead gorgeous as Carly. Little did he know, but Carly wasn't ready to share any of it with any boy, regardless of how hot he might be. And Randy Strongbow was all of that.

"Does your mom know we're going up to the burial grounds?" Maggie asked, suspecting correctly that there was something more to it.

Carly frowned. With an eye to the sliding-glass doors and her voice lowered, she said, "I told her we were going to be hanging out with some friends. You know, do something normal. She kind of gets uptight with the burial ground thing. My grandmother is like that, too. You don't mess with the spirit world, don't mention the dead. Stuff like that. If I asked her to take us over to the Hastings' place, she'd be asking all kinds of questions all the way there—if we even got that far. I know for sure she wouldn't let me go. So, I asked Randy to take us." Carly held up her cellphone. "He's leaving his house right now."

Maggie was concerned when Katy saw Randy, that she might have something to say. Maybe that Maggie wasn't taking things seriously.

But Katy did nothing of the sort. Instead, she said she was actually glad to see such a strapping young man. She then asked him if he could handle a gun.

HUNGRY

Randy answered by saying he had done lots of hunting. "I have two rifles of my own. My father has a bunch more."

That's when Katy left the three of them alone there in the parlor for a moment, returning with an impressive and seemingly newer model shotgun. It kind of surprised them.

She extended it out towards Randy. "I suppose you know how to use this, then?"

Randy took the weapon and immediately checked the safety.

Katy nodded her approval.

"Are we expecting trouble?" Randy asked, putting the shotgun to his side, barrel to the floor.

Katy shook her head. There was no expression of concern upon her face or in her eyes. "We are going up into the hills at night where we'll be trespassing upon critter territory. There are four shells in that there thing, one already chambered. Coyotes get a little too curious, a round of buckshot in their relative vicinity will send them running."

Carly looked less than thrilled. "There's going to be coyotes?"

Katy laughed, all in good fun. "My dear, there's always coyotes. Most times they keep to themselves. There's plenty of mice and the like up where we're going. Coyotes hunt at night. Put two and two together, and any way you look at it, you get four."

Carly's expression didn't change. "So, there's going to be coyotes?"

Randy lifted the gun a tad. "You just stick really close to me, Carly."

Maggie had to give Randy credit for seeing the 'in' and jumping on it. "Yeah, Carly," she said. "He's got a big gun and everything." She smiled at the unintended entendre.

HUNGRY

The Burial Grounds

The two females of the clan could feel that something was wrong. It was instinctual. It had nothing to do with the length of time that the males were gone. The alpha routinely took them off on hunts lasting much longer. Prey wasn't always easy to find, and then once found, it had to be taken.

No, this was something different.

There was an absence to their collective scent, not just the thinning that came with distance. Distant or not, there was always something fresh to trace, some more recent redolence to replace that which time and the elements had swept away.

Every action had its own scent. There was a scent for marking territory, sprayed where it was likely to linger, sheltered from the elements. There was a scent for sentry duty in which the males would scout the perimeter, reestablishing the clan's presence and checking for trespassers. There was a scent for coupling. There was a scent for disagreement. There was a scent for hunger, for contentment. There was a scent for danger, for the hunt, and for returning from the hunt—both successfully and not.

But here, now, there was only the scent of marking, that and, perhaps, what lingered in the wake of departure.

The two females exchanged glances. The communication between them was brief, but understood. The older of the two, taking the initiative, stepped away from the small chamber and in the direction of the tunnel leading out.

The young male was there as if waiting. It would be natural for him to expect to lead. But the older female stopped him with a low hiss.

HUNGRY

Inexperienced, it had no effect on him. He moved around her and managed to get a stride out ahead.

The older female reached out and across his face. With an effortless stroke, as if swimming in a quiet pool, she swept him back, taking him off his feet, and dumping him on his backside to the ground.

The young male had not expected that she'd dare, and despite his surprise and indignation, sprung to his feet in a single motion and came back at her.

She, too, had already turned, sinking at the knees into an aggressive stance and with both hands loose at her side.

The musk she exuded left little room for doubt on the part of the young male. He relented, relaxing his posture, but his eyes fixed upon the significantly larger female. It was a fight he wouldn't win. She wouldn't try to kill him, but she would make it hurt.

Message delivered, the female started again to move up the tunnel, not bothering to give the young male another look.

There at the entrance, standing back deep enough into the darkness as not to expose herself to predators—there were always predators, she tilted and turned her head, first this way and then that, sniffing and tasting the air. Nothing but that which had already began to fade.

She crouched down so there'd be less to see of her. Staying close to the ground and near to the rock, she moved out into the open. She fixed her sight first to the lay of land straight out ahead, allowing her eyes to adjust to the shades of grey and black where she was accustomed to only shades of amber, then to the finer details.

Her sense of depth in focus, she slowly scanned the space between the trees there at the end of the relatively open ground

169

before her. Marching steadily downhill, it wasn't long before the tangle of branches and treetops turned everything a curtain of trembling grey, lighter shades to the top where it all gave way to the sky, and darker the lower and deeper her eyes focused.

That's when she caught the scent of prey. Suddenly, she was overwhelmingly aware of her own hunger. She had not eaten in near two days, and even then, only the meager slivers of meat the males had brought to be shared among the young male, the other female, the newborn, and herself.

Females of the clan, too, could hunt. Not as efficiently as the alpha-led males. But then again, their need wasn't as great. The alpha fed the clan. The females simply satisfied immediate need in the interim.

The elder female moved cautiously away from the barrow, keeping to the shadows of the early nightfall and towards the cover of the tree line. She'd not hunt on her own, but instead was seeking out a more certain direction and some sense of her prey. Once determined, she'd signal for the younger female to join her.

She knew the scent from the flesh upon which she had most recently fed. The texture felt strange in her mouth, the taste unfamiliar on her tongue. But it sated her appetite, and for now that would do. Lifting her head, her face and nose angled up, she breathed deeply and slowly, tasting the thin traces of scent which managed to elude the sweeping breeze coming down the hill at her back. But it was enough for her to be certain the was prey nearby.

Looking about to make sure she herself was not being stalked, she turned back and quickly and soundlessly returned to the barrow.

Randy's 4X4 had no trouble negotiating the narrow dirt road which ran up the hill and up into the burial grounds. To get to it, he had to leave Sylvan Road to the north and west of the Aloise house was. The unpaved road cut back into the trees, and then ran, at the same time, both across and up the hill. Muddy from the light rains which had been falling on and off for the last two days, the traction remained fairly solid, the vehicle's heavy-duty suspension brushing off the sudden dips and bumps with little inconvenience to all inside.

Katy Hastings had a particular spot in mind which she preferred for the placement of the pots. It required a little extra walking, she told them, but the trail was less steep than the other ways up to the grounds and a lot clearer. No worry about tripping over unexpected rocks and roots or stumbling into ditches and ruts. They'd be carrying clay pots and candles, she reminded them. Adding that it would do no good to smash one or the other before they got to where they were going.

On the way over to Katy's house, Maggie had cautioned both Randy and Carly about mentioning anything about partying up the hill or fooling around in the burial grounds. "It's not like she doesn't know every kid in the Valley goes up there, but this is serious stuff to her, and I kind of want to get it right myself."

"I think," said Randy, after declaring himself cool with it, "that when my time comes—and that's if I'm still around here, I'd want someone to do this for me, too."

Carly agreed. "It is part of our tradition, part of who we are."

Maggie chuckled. "Look at us, going all Native."

"You have to admit," said Randy, taking his eyes momentarily from the road to meet Maggie's in the rearview mirror. "It's kind of spooky up there, especially at night. Not like there are ghosts or anything like that, but there's definitely something."

Before Maggie could answer, Carly said, "Yeah, like three-hundred years of dead people."

HUNGRY

Randy corrected her. "No one's been buried there like in a hundred years. And it's not quite three-hundred. More like two-hundred-fifty."

Carly stuck her tongue out at him, but his eyes were by then back on the road. The turn-off to Katy's house was coming up. "Okay, *Big Ben*. But you know what I mean. Everyone in our lifetime, and for generations back, have been buried down here in the cemetery. There are headstones going back to like 1915 or something. If there's anything spooky up in the burial grounds, it's not ghosts or spirits of the dead."

Randy clucked. "Oh yeah? Then what is it?"

Carly looked over her shoulder at Maggie in the back seat before answering. "Maybe you should ask Katy," she said to Randy. "She's the expert. Maybe it is portals, things like that, and shadow walkers or Holy People."

On the ride up to the burial grounds, Randy had thought to ask. But besides a little small talk between Katy and the girls, the opportunity didn't present itself.

And then they were where they were headed.

Having reached the spot Katy was looking for, she tapped Randy's hand on the steering wheel and told him to pull over. He didn't want to leave the 4X4 blocking the road, so pulled it off to the right and onto a somewhat open patch of long grass bowed from the weight of the rain.

Katy wasn't so pleased with having to step down into the small muddied puddle just outside her side of the vehicle, but as she was wearing the appropriate footwear, and was bound to get muddy regardless, it was quickly dismissed.

Maggie and Carly each carried one of the clay pots Katy had made and decorated. Maggie had her mother's. Carly had Andy's.

172

HuNGRY

Each also carried a candle consisting of paraffin melted and poured into a small, thin glass into which was inserted a sturdy wick. Randy had the shotgun. Katy had a small drum, covered with the skin of an animal, and a ceremonial drumstick, made of deer bone, the rounded head covered with deer skin, also.

"Remember what I told you," reminded Katy before they set off. "Once we get up there, pick a spot in the area I show you that feels right. If you're quiet, it'll come to you. Put the clay jar where the rock runs flat, the part that looks like the church altar. That's where the spirit path lies. Then find a place close-by where you can set the candle so the wind won't blow it out, and then light it. I'm going to have to go off a bit. There's a special spot from where I can call to your mother and brother, so that they can hear me. Wait until you hear me chanting and the beating of the drum before you light the candles. The flames will draw them near, and then they'll find the pots. But we'll have to leave before then or they won't come."

The trail up to the burial grounds wasn't the one the teens knew. This one was narrow and pretty much overgrown with grass and mats of low growing tangles with small round and white flowers, all of which were fading into shades of grey now that the sun had gone down below the tree tops to the west.

"You guys probably didn't even know this trail was here, did you? You all go up the other way."

The three young people exchanged glances.

"I'm not that old," laughed Katy. "I was your age once, too. And that burial ground has been there a lot longer than any of us."

That was Randy's in. "Is it really haunted, Katy...I mean Ms. Hastings?"

"You can call me Katy, Randy." She paused. "Haunted is not the right word. Spiritual. It is a very spiritual place. Our people

173

chose it for a reason. You don't put a burial ground any old random place. The Medicine Man, Shaman if you want—the tribe's spiritual leader, has to know just the right place. He goes out on his own into the woods, or the mountains, or the desert, wherever it might be. Then there's the trance, brought on by the herbs, by some traditional concoction only he or she knows. The Medicine Man's spirit leaves his body, while the body stays in place, and goes up to the planes of the Holy People, to the Great Spirit, and it is only then the burial ground is chosen."

Randy had heard similar lore before. They all had. But it was kind of cool and different coming from Katy. "You're a Shaman...our Shaman, isn't that right, Katy?"

Katy stopped walking for a moment. Turned to face the three teens. "My father was the Shaman for the people here in the Valley, our Medicine Man, as was his father before that, and his before that. I had no intention of keeping it in the family, as it were. But as my father had no sons, it was kind of handed down despite what I wanted. It was something that kind of happened on its own, and yes, when my father passed, the people here in the Valley naturally assumed the responsibility was mine. So, yes. I'm the tribal Shaman. As you know. The role is different these days, what with modern technology and people like Dr. Dave, and your mom, too, Maggie. Nonetheless, as long as I'm able, our people will have all the guidance I can give to see them along the road of the dead."

"We were kind of talking about that on the way over," said Randy. "So, what happens when you're gone, I mean, for the rest of us? Who's going to show the way?"

Carly thought to slap Randy's arm or something, but her hands were full. Instead, she nudged him in the ribs with a sharp elbow.

"What?" He asked. "We were, weren't we?"

HUNGRY

Katy took no offense. Why would she? It was a natural question. "Well," she said. "We're just going to have to find us someone here in the Valley who's interested in keeping old traditions alive." She already had Elena Torres in mind. "But for now, we had better be about our business, or it's going to get too dark to be stumbling around up here and not see where we're going."

The two clan females had made their way down the hill only a short distance before the scent became richer, more telling. Not too far now, they could feel it.

But before they could take another step, either one of them, there came a new scent drifting over to them from the trees to their right. It too was strong, and much more feral. There was no missing its predatory nature.

As one, they moved to nearby trees and crouched low using the thin branches and small leaves as cover, the brush growing closer to the ground to mute their movement. There was no need for the females to communicate. They knew the direction from which the predators were coming. Their eyes were trained to the same spot.

Out into the clearing stepped first the large male coyote. He, too, was on a scent. It had been strong, but just then his questing nose couldn't quite find it. The other two males came up behind him, neither quite so big, but big enough that the three together were a competent force.

The two females from the clan held their ground, neither moving in the slightest.

Off to the west, the sky had gotten very dark.

Then, just as suddenly as they had appeared, the three coyotes went on their way, trotting off into the tree line and downhill.

HUNGRY

The two clan females waited, allowing the coyotes to move off. No longer sensing any threat, they, too, started downhill.

They didn't have to go too far.

Having come to the altar-like run of stones, raised from the ground and tilting ever so perceptively one past the other, they stopped, concealing themselves alongside the trunks of the trees to the uphill side. The scent of prey was strong.

There to the other side of the rocks, the older of the two females spotted movement. It was grey against grey, but there was no mistaken what it was.

The younger female came up close to her side, and together they watched.

A second target came into their line of sight. It moved upright and unaware. But it was slightly further away than the first one, and there was a line of rocks to get past.

As they positioned themselves, ready to pounce, a sudden rhythmic pounding bounced off the surface of the stone, taking the two female clan members by surprise. Barely suppressing their flight response, they instead scurried back into the cover of the trees.

Crouching down low to the ground and back out of sight, they were then aware of another sound. It was steady and musical, calm and at the same time with presence. It drew them from their place of concealment and back towards the rocks.

There they stood in place for a brief period, listening and watching as the upright figures, smocked in grey, moved about but a few lengths away. Gradually, and rather quickly, any threat the females were feeling had faded. Whatever was making the sounds, there was no portent of danger.

HUNGRY

The instinct to hunt peaking, the elder female started to creep forward, the younger one leaving her side and moving left to circle around.

Just then came a single glare of fiery light, and then another, brief streaks of lightning which flared out across their line of sight and washed away the dark. Blinded, the females halted and recoiled, not tall but erect and exposed upon the heights of the rock.

Off to their right, there was a low and menacing growl. It was the alpha coyote. He had led the other males, following the trail of the scent. But breaking from the trees, they turned away from the females and toward something they had learned to fear.

Randy heard the large coyote before he actually saw it. Turning towards the surprised growl, he pointed the shotgun and fired. His aim was hurried. He heard the buckshot spray across the stone. The big coyote yipped. Turn and ran, heading back into the trees.

It was only then that Randy saw the other two coyotes. He steadied the barrel of the shotgun and pulled the trigger, the roar drowning out the two successive barks of a hunting rifle, sharp and clean, which came from behind him. Then came two more. These he heard.

The elder female saw the first flash from the hunting rifle. It was intense and bright. Her instincts failed her. Frozen, she failed to react. Crouched but exposed, the second bullet exploded into her narrow chest. The blow was sudden and unexpected, and then she toppled off the rock into a narrow space below.

The younger female fell in much the same way. The first shot caught her in the upper leg. She turned instinctively to run for the cover of the trees. As she did, the second shot ripped through her upper back, crashed into the dense bone at her sternum, was redirected, and came out a fist-sized hole to the left of her abdomen. She, too, was dead before she hit the ground.

HUNGRY

A Question of Sovereignty

Sheriff Hardy had always planned on a town meeting, eventually.

However, as the news spread that there were two more of the creatures killed the previous night, the sheriff had no choice but to get ahead of things. He arranged with Father Jacob to use the church rectory, and then had Tanya send out the email using the same emergency communication system used to let parents know of snow days, school lockdowns or even local fundraisers. He also made sure that his deputies got out some fliers, tacking them to the telephone poles, the community events showcase in town, and giving them to the local merchants to display on their countertops.

The rectory was standing room only.

The sheriff had asked his son, Robert, to be there, and to bring Joy with him. He wanted both to say a little something to the community, allay any fears or concerns, and make it all sound kind of intellectual and scientific. "We don't want anybody taking this to the next level." He didn't say what that next level was, but Robert and Joy had a general idea.

He had also outlined brief roles for Father Jacob and Dr. Dave. Each was asked to say a few words. "Keep to the script," he told them.

Once everyone had settled into the neatly arranged folding chairs, and others had found a place along the walls or to the back of the rectory, Sheriff Hardy came up to the dais and clicked on the mic. The others were seated behind him.

Hardy started by welcoming everyone, looking around the room to see if there was anyone significant by absence. But it seemed that outside of the youngest children, most of the

179

community was concerned or interested enough to hear what was going to be said.

"Let me start by saying," Hardy began, "that this is truly a very sad time for us all. We are a very close community. To lose four of our loved ones and friends so unexpectedly, so suddenly, and in such a disturbing way, is very hard to internalize, very hard to understand. I wish I had words for it, and I'm thankful that we have among us others that are much better at that sort of thing than I." He turned to look towards Father Jacob and Dr. Dave.

He continued. "I had hoped to have more time before we got together like this. I realize you all have so many questions, and I had hoped to have the answers to those questions. That two more of these animals were shot and killed last night obligated me to move things forward. So here we are."

All had agreed during the preparation meeting that they'd refer to the others as *animals*. It'd be easier for the community to deal with and to make sense of things.

"For those of you who might not have heard., my son Robert and Father Jacob shot two more of the animals before they had the chance to attack Ms. Hastings and three of our young people who were up in the burial grounds to perform a ceremony.

"Thankfully, no one was hurt, and we are quite confident that there are no more of these animals up the Hill or anywhere else in the Valley. Just to be sure, we have organized a search party and will be going out following this meeting. We are going to cover every inch of the Valley."

There were quite a few nodding heads towards the front of the room, all of whom were community members who had volunteered to come along. Bob Aloise was among them.

Taking advantage of the momentary pause, Mike Zink, a community member whose head was not nodding, called out,

"What exactly are we dealing with here, Sheriff? Some kind of monster?"

It was not the kind of word Hardy had wanted to hear, but it also wasn't unexpected. "Mike," he said, "I'm going to let someone a lot more knowledgeable when it comes to animals answer that question." He turned towards Joy and invited her up to the dais.

As she approached to stand beside him, Sheriff Hardy introduced her. "This here is Dr. Joy Martin. Dr. Martin is a zoologist from Cornell University, and a close friend of my son Robert. She, with the assistance of Dr. Dave, has done a thorough examination of the animals, and is here to tell you what she can about them."

Joy preferred that Hardy would have chosen some other word than 'thorough', but he met her objection with the need to play to community emotions and concerns. Using that particular word, he insisted, would give the impression that what they were being told was good, solid information.

Joy was quite accustomed to speaking to audiences. The difference was, though, usually that audience was made up of other like-minded or similarly experienced professionals or, on the either end of the spectrum, school children. These people weren't here to be entertained, or brought up to date on the latest theories. They wanted to know what it was that killed their friends and family. They wanted to leave assured that the danger had been eliminated. They wanted the peace of mind that comes with a rational and logical explanation.

She didn't have one.

She knew also what it was that was expected of her.

After providing an informal sketch of her credentials, Joy nodded towards Sheriff Hardy. Sheriff Hardy than proceeded to his laptop which he had set up ahead of time. He hit enter on the keyboard and the screen on the wall above their heads came alive with an image of one of the male creatures. There was a collective gasp from the community, followed by a cacophony of comments and exclamation.

Joy waited for the excitement to die down and then started. It took a few moments before she had their attention, her first words probably lost on most. "We completed a full autopsy on one of the animals, and less involved procedures on the others. Leaving out the gory details, we know the following: They are anthropomorphic, which means they move upright on two legs like us. The characteristics of the feet are unlike those of the hands. This is something not normally encountered in nature, unless you consider birds and some prehistoric dinosaur-like creatures. The feet are more like that of goats, camels, pigs, and hippos—species of that kind, while the hands are more like those of chimpanzees. They have opposable thumbs and elongated fingers. Not all that much different than us. The nails, however, are significantly more like those of large cats, or even bears. Definitely those of a predator-like animal. The largest of the animals is 63 inches tall and approximately ninety pounds. It is male. There are four other males, each averaging 61 inches and about 85 pounds. There are two females. They are both 58 inches in height and about 80 pounds. All of the animals are fully covered head to toe with hair. The hair is short and has a velvet-like consistency. All of the animals are a tawny color, much like a mountain lion, though perhaps slightly paler and a bit more to the yellow end of the prism. The facial features are somewhat canine, though less pronounced, especially with regard to the snout or muzzle—not as elongated or with as much depth. The teeth are limited to canines and incisors, ideal for ripping and tearing. There

HUNGRY

are no molars, suggestive of a primarily carnivorous diet. The eyes, similar to other animals, lack sclera—the white of the eyes. That area is instead a pale amber. The pupils are black and enlarged in color. They give no indication of dilation, meaning they are not designed to respond to a well-lighted environment, which would explain why they were active at night and not during the daylight hours. Finally, they have smaller ears and a relatively underdeveloped sense of hearing. Asked my professional opinion, I would classify them as mammals, but I would not put them in any specific classification of mammal."

"So, what are you saying?" Called out Mike Zink. "Or don't you know?"

Joy had no intention of being misleading or lying. "At this time, no. This is not an animal I have come across before. That said, it shares many characteristics of animals we do know well, as well as sharing some of our own. For me, that is enough to suggest it may be simply a hereunto unencountered species of primate. It may be a question of evolution, or lack thereof. It is also possibly a mutation."

The locals had by then, passively and collectively, accepted Zink as their spokesman. They were looking in his direction, anticipating he'd go on.

He didn't disappoint. "Fair enough, Dr. Martin. Two questions: First, why *unencountered* and why now? Second, a possible mutation from what?"

Before answering, Joy turned to exchange glances with both Robert and Sheriff Hardy. Father and son then looked at each other, exchanged non-verbal agreement, after which the sheriff nodded that she should go on.

Joy said, "We as zoologists are discovering new species here on Earth almost on a daily basis. Generally, such discoveries occur

183

when we move into less explored territories—deep seas, for example, or the species itself moves from isolation into a more exposed environment. Climate change, for example, may have something to do with it, shrinking the species' environment, limiting its food source, something, for which it is required to move, to expand its territory. An animal like this one, for all we know, has been existing up in these hills for years, hundreds of years, without exposing itself or having cause to wander from where it felt safe. It can be something as basic as getting lost.

"In terms of mutation: I only offered that as a possibility. If pressed on the issue, I would say, I see no other species than primate from which this one would have mutated or evolved. Evolution is generally seen as an environmental response, equipped to survive. In that regard, this particular unfamiliar species would do well in most of the environs we have here on Earth, but does not seem to be designed for any one in particular. Which is not normal. As for mutations: A mutation would still have at its base something recognized from the original. Godzilla, fictional as he is, is a mutation. You yet see something of the dinosaur in him. I can't say much of certainty about these animals."

When Joy paused, the attention of the locals again was directed to Mike Zink.

"We appreciate your candor, Dr. Martin. One more thing, then. Are you suggesting something alien or, dare I say, supernatural?"

This, too, was a question well-anticipated. Joy smiled, not from humor, but for validation. "That's a question best answered by Dr. Hardy." She then turned and gestured him to the dais.

Robert didn't require any introduction. He was both well-known and respected. He started with a general greeting and added how good it felt to be back in the Valley. It was genuine. He then acknowledged the community's heritage and ancestry, taking the position that there was validity in traditional lore.

"I'm an anthropologist," he reminded them, "and a bit of a paleoanthropologist, at that. For those of you less familiar, that's to say that I have a pronounced interest in prehistoric cultures and those of early human beings. While most of the world would like to believe that we as humans are required to trace our origins on this planet to the Middle East, I'll remind you that the earliest human remains here in North America go back eight-thousand years, well before the pyramids.

"So, what am I getting at? What I'm getting at is that our culture as Native Americans is derived from ancestors that go back many millennia. What we hold as our tradition and lore is based on the experiences and values of those ancestors, passed on one generation to the next. And it is not just the Iroquois. Whether it's the lands which now make up Florida, or those that we call Utah, Arizona, New Mexico, and, too, all of Mexico, Central America, South America, and even the frozen tundra of the utmost northern reaches of Canada and Alaska, all the indigenous peoples reference different kinds of entities and spirits, all with supernatural qualities.

"While I'm not saying these entities and spirits are anything more than an attempt to explain what was then unexplainable, I am saying that in all likelihood their manifestation—what they look like—was all based on some animal or beast that was very real.

"Take the wendigo. Who here hasn't heard stories? And what is a wendigo but a human being transformed as a result of consuming human flesh. A perverse mashup of those characteristics we most fear in predatory beasts, such as claws and fangs, and other things that would scare or horrify us. The same is true of the Skinwalker, werewolves, demons, even the Chupacabra.

Always ugly, fearsome, scary, anything that would feed into our natural fears and discourage us from participating in the behavior associated with such transformation or fate.

"My point is that it is quite possible that what we have here in these animals is a later-day version of the same type of odd and isolated creatures which occasionally revealed themselves to our ancestors, and which served as the image to give shape and form to taboo and superstition.

"Finally, as I have told my father, Dr. Martin and I will return to the university where we can take advantage of extensive resources to do an exhaustive search using the information we have gathered. I promise you that once we have done so that I will get a full report to my father, and then he that information to all of you."

He waited for questions.

Mike Zink looked once around the room, saw the eyes upon him. "It almost sounds, Robert, like you're talking about a Sasquatch, or something like that."

"I'm only suggesting, Mike," Robert said, "that all legend is based on reality to some degree. There is no getting around the fact that we have eight very real animals here in our lab which killed four community members here in the valley. These animals are not Coyotes, wolves, mountain lions, or bears. They are not human, and definitely not any species that I know of, nor does Dr. Martin—a clear expert on the subject." He smiled at Joy. "Nor are they spirit or demon or alien."

Zink interrupted. "How do you know they're not alien, Robert? Aren't there rock paintings and etchings out west that some interpret as alien visitors, with what look to be helmets and oxygen lines or breathing tubes of some sort?"

HUNGRY

Robert acknowledged Mike's observation. He then said, "Logical supposition only, Mike. Dr. Dave and Dr. Martin could both speak more knowledgeably on the subject than I, but it has to do with the brain. While my understanding is there are some indications of superior development when compared to other mammals, meaning not us, it still lacks the capacity to engage in advanced cognitive performance. In other words, incapable of the types of technological leaps that would be required for space travel. If that's where you want to go with this." He shrugged.

"So, unless you're prepared to go with a *Planet of the Apes* theory, or perhaps a Stephen King meteor, I'm not sure what to tell you, any of you. As a scientist, I'm required to be systematic and logical. I'm doing the best I can."

When Robert had finished, Sheriff Hardy called upon Dr. Dave and the two of them went up to the dais together. Sheriff Hardy then explained that each of the animals had been cremated and their ashes discarded. Before any questions could be asked, Hardy handed the microphone over to Dr. Dave.

"After lengthy discussion over possible actions, I recommended to Sheriff Hardy that the remains be destroyed," he said. "My concern was for any possible disease they might be carrying. Animals in the wild are often carrying parasites and vermin, whether upon their bodies or internally. While we'd have little to fear from either of these, there is also the possibility of virus or bacteria. Since we can't say with any certainty where these animals came from, it is better to error on the side of caution. The only way to be certain was to incinerate the bodies and thereby eliminate anything that might be of potential danger to us."

By this time, it was expected that Mike Zink would say something. He felt it, too. "Dave, while we all appreciate you looking out for us, and none of us have any objection with the cremating of these animals; nevertheless, I have to ask, if these animals are local—perhaps that's not the right word, wouldn't it be logical to assume that anything they might carry in the way of the things you mention would be something we've probably already been exposed to, one way or the other?"

Dave pressed his lips tight. "We've all been exposed to mosquitos, Mike. But that doesn't protect us from the Zika virus, or explain where that virus came from." He hesitated, then taking a quick glance over at Sheriff Hardy, he added, "And it is possible they aren't from around here."

A murmur of surprise passed through the crowd, like a sudden breeze through the tree tops.

Mike nodded. "Point taken, Dave."

Here, the sheriff took the opportunity to move the meeting to its conclusion. "I want to remind you all of our sovereignty," he said, a point of significance to everyone there. "The last thing we need is outsiders descending upon us, whether its authorities from one level or another, scientists, or so-called investigators chasing after ETs, UFOs, and other boogey-man-like entities.

"I'm confident we have the right people right here in this room to make sure we get all the answers we need."

The sheriff then turned to Father Jacob, asked him if he had anything to add.

Father Jacob came to the sheriff's side and was handed the microphone.

"I just want everyone to know that there will be mass tonight at 8:00. I'm sure at a times like these, we can all draw strength as we gather together in the house of the Lord, from His Word and from prayer. We may not know God's plan, but together we can take consolation in His promise of the Peace and Serenity that are sure to follow."

HUNGRY

The young male put himself between the three coyotes and the newborn. The newborn was backed up to the far wall of the shallow chamber, up on both feet, lips drawn back and teeth bared.

The large alpha coyote was being cautious. The multiple smells twitching his nostrils served to momentarily confuse him, to make him wary.

The young male of the clan attacked.

Instinctively, all three coyotes sprang back.

ABOUT THE AUTHOR

The author currently lives on Long Island's south shore. He continues to explore the paranormal and the randomness of the existence which we as human beings share.

Made in the USA
Middletown, DE
28 June 2022